"Tristan!" Ivy cried out loud. "Are you there?"

Ivy stared down at the pool water streaked and spangled by the fluorescent lights. She would never love the water the way Tristan had, but this was where he had first reached out to her. This was where she had to try to reach back to him.

"Tristan?" she whispered.

The only sound was the steady buzzing of the fluorescent lights.

Angels, help me! Help me reach him.

"Tristan!" Ivy cried out loud. "Are you there?"

Ivy dropped her head. He wasn't there. He couldn't hear her. She took a step back from the edge. When she turned around, she gasped.

Behind her the air shimmered. It was like liquid light—a gold stem burning in the rough shape of a person. The glowing shape was surrounded by a mist of sheer and trembling colors.

"Tristan," she said softly. She reached out her hand and started walking toward him. She longed to be enveloped by his golden light, surrounded by the colors, embraced by all that Tristan was now.

Don't miss the other two books
in this exciting trilogy:

Volume I: *Kissed by an Angel*
Volume II: *The Power of Love*

Available from ARCHWAY Paperbacks

KISSED BY AN ANGEL

SOULMATES

Elizabeth Chandler

AN ARCHWAY PAPERBACK
Published by POCKET BOOKS
New York   London   Toronto   Sydney   Tokyo   Singapore

AN ARCHWAY PAPERBACK *Original*

An Archway Paperback published by
POCKET BOOKS, a division of Simon & Schuster Inc.
1230 Avenue of the Americas, New York, NY 10020

Produced by Daniel Weiss Associates, Inc., New York

ISBN: 0-671-89147-2

First Archway Paperback printing September 1995

10 9 8 7 6 5 4 3 2 1

AN ARCHWAY PAPERBACK and colophon are registered trademarks of Simon & Schuster Inc.

Printed in the U.S.A.

IL 7+

1

With her chin held high and her cloud of curly blond hair tossed back from her face, Ivy shut the school counselor's door and walked down the hall. Several guys from the swim team turned to stare as she moved toward her locker. Ivy forced herself to return their glances and to look confident. The pants and top she wore for the first day of the school year had been selected by Suzanne, her oldest friend and fashion expert. Too bad Suzanne didn't pick out a matching bag to go over my head, Ivy thought. She walked past the senior class bulletin board. People whispered. People pointed her out with small nods. She should have expected it.

Anyone whom Tristan Carruthers had fallen for would be pointed out. Anyone who had been with Tristan the night he was killed would be whispered about. So naturally, anyone who had tried to kill herself because she couldn't get over Tristan's death would be pointed to and whispered about and watched very, very carefully. And that was what everyone said about Ivy: brokenhearted, she had taken some pills, then tried to throw herself in front of a train.

She could remember only the brokenhearted part, the long summer after the car accident, the nightmares with the deer crashing through the windshield. Three weeks ago she'd had another of her nightmares and had woken up screaming. All she could recall from that night was being comforted by her stepbrother, Gregory, then falling asleep, looking at Tristan's photo. That photo, her favorite picture of Tristan, in which he was wearing his old school jacket and a baseball cap backward on his head, haunted her now. It had haunted her even before she'd heard her little brother's strange account of that night.

Philip's story of an angel saving her hadn't convinced her family or the police that this wasn't a suicide attempt. And how could she deny taking a drug that had shown up in the hospital's blood tests? How could she argue against the train engineer's statement to the police that he wouldn't have been able to stop in time?

"Chick, chick, chick." A soft quivering voice interrupted Ivy's thoughts. "Who wants to play chick, chick, chick?"

He was calling to her from the shadowy space beneath the stairs. Ivy knew it was Gregory's best friend, Eric Ghent. She kept on walking.

"Chick, chick, chick . . ."

When she didn't react he emerged from the dark stairwell, looking like a skeleton startled out of his tomb. His wispy blond hair lay in strings across his high forehead, and his eyes looked like pale blue marbles set in bony sockets. Ivy had not seen Eric for the last three weeks; she suspected that Gregory had kept his jeering friend away from her.

Now Eric moved quickly enough to block her path. "Why *didn't* you do it?" he asked. "Lose your nerve? Why didn't you go ahead and kill yourself?"

"Disappointed?" Ivy asked back.

"Chick, chick, chick," he said softly, tauntingly.

"Leave me alone, Eric." Ivy walked faster.

"Uh-uh. Not now." He grabbed her wrist, his thin fingers wrapping tightly around her arm. "You can't blow me off now, Ivy. You and I have too much in common."

"We have nothing in common," she replied, pulling away from him.

"Gregory," he said, tapping one of his fingers. "Drugs." He ticked off a second item. "And we're both champions of the game of chicken." He grabbed a third finger and wiggled it. "We're buddies now."

Ivy kept walking, though she wanted to run. Eric bobbed along with her.

"Tell your good buddy," he said, "what made you want to do it? What were you thinking when you saw that train rushing down the track at you? Were you stoked? What kind of trip was it?"

Ivy felt repulsed by his questions. It seemed impossible to think she would have deliberately jumped in front of the train. She had lost Tristan, but there were still people in her life she cared deeply about—Philip, her mother, Suzanne and Beth, and Gregory, who had protected her and comforted her after Tristan's death. Gregory had been through a lot himself, his mother having committed suicide the month before Tristan died. Ivy had seen the pain and anger caused by that death, and it seemed totally crazy to her that she would try the same thing.

But everyone said she had. Gregory said so.

"How many times do I have to tell you? I can't remember what happened that night, Eric. I can't."

"But you will," he said with a quiet laugh. "Sooner or later, you will."

Then he stepped away from her and turned back, like a dog that had reached the end of its territory. Ivy continued toward her and her friends' lockers, ignoring more curious stares. She hoped that Suzanne and Beth were finished with their senior orientation meetings.

Ivy didn't need to look at the locker numbers to find Suzanne Goldstein's new nesting place. Suzanne wasn't there, but the locker was being fumigated with an open bottle of her favorite perfume, which guided Ivy—and all guys interested in leaving Suzanne a note—directly to the spot. Suzanne had found three new guys to date recently, but Beth and Ivy knew it was just a ploy to make Gregory jealous.

Beth Van Dyke's locker, which was close to Ivy's this

year, already had a piece of paper sticking out of it, but it probably wasn't a note from an admiring hunk. More likely, she had shut the door on a scrap of a steamy romance, one of the many that filled her notebooks.

Ivy went ahead to her own locker to drop off her new books. Kneeling down, she dialed the combination and pulled open the door. She gasped. Taped inside her door was a photograph of Tristan, the same picture that had haunted her for the past three weeks. For a moment she couldn't breathe. How had it gotten there?

Frantically she recalled everything she had done that morning: roll call in homeroom, then a general assembly, then the school store, and finally a meeting with the counselor. She ran over the list twice, but she couldn't remember taping the photo to the door. Was she really losing her mind?

Ivy closed her eyes and leaned against the door. I'm crazy, she thought. I'm really crazy.

"Am I nuts, Gregory?" she had asked three weeks earlier as she stood in her bedroom on her first day home from the hospital. She held Tristan's photograph in her trembling hands. Gregory gently took the picture away from her, giving it to Philip, her nine-year-old savior.

"You're going to get better, Ivy. That much I'm sure of," Gregory said, drawing her down on the bed next to him, putting his arm around her.

"Meaning I'm crazy now."

Gregory didn't answer right away. She had noticed

5

the change in him when he came to see her at the hospital. His dark hair was combed perfectly, as always, and his handsome face was like a mask, just as it had been when she first met him, his light gray eyes hiding his deepest thoughts.

"It's a hard thing to understand, Ivy," he said carefully. "It's hard to know exactly what you were thinking at the time." He glanced over at Philip, who was setting the framed photo on the bureau. "And Philip's story sure doesn't help much."

Her brother responded with a stubborn glare.

"Maybe now that no one else is around, you can tell us what really happened, Philip," Gregory said.

Philip glanced up at the two empty shelves where Ivy's collection of angels had once stood. He had the statues now. Ivy had given them to him on the condition that he would never again talk about angels.

"I already told you."

"Try again," Gregory said, his voice low and tense.

"Please, Philip." Ivy reached out for his hand. "It'll help me."

He let her hold his hand loosely. She knew he was tired of being interrogated, first by the police, then by the doctors at the hospital, then by their mother and Gregory's father, Andrew.

"I was sleeping," Philip told her. "After you had your nightmare, Gregory said he'd stay with you. I was asleep again. But then I heard somebody calling me. I didn't know who it was at first. He told me to wake up. He said you needed help."

Philip stopped, as if that were the end of the story. "And?"

He glanced up at the empty shelves, then pulled away from her.

"Go on," Ivy prompted.

"You're just going to yell at me."

"No, I won't," she said. "And neither will Gregory." She gave Gregory a warning look. "Just tell us what you remember."

"You heard a voice in your head," Gregory said, "and it was telling you that Ivy needed help. The voice sounded something like Tristan's."

"It *was* Tristan," Philip insisted. "It was angel Tristan!"

"Okay, okay," Gregory said.

"Did this voice tell you why I was in trouble?" Ivy asked. "Did the voice tell you where I was?"

He shook his head. "Tristan said to put on my shoes, go down the stairs, and go out the back door. Then we ran across the yard to the stone wall. I knew I wasn't supposed to go over it, but Tristan said it was okay because he was with me."

Ivy could feel Gregory's body tense next to hers, but she nodded encouragingly to Philip.

"It was scary, Ivy, climbing down the ridge. It was hard to hold on. The rocks were real slippery."

"It's impossible," Gregory said, sounding frustrated and perplexed. "A kid couldn't have done it. *I* couldn't have done it."

"I had Tristan with me," Philip reminded him.

"I don't know how you got to the station, Philip," Gregory said heatedly, "but I'm tired of this Tristan story. I don't want to hear it again."

"I do," Ivy said quietly, and heard Gregory draw in his breath. "Go on," she said.

"When we got to the bottom, we still had to get over another fence. I asked what was going on, but Tristan wouldn't tell me. He just said we had to help you. So I started climbing, then I kind of messed up. I thought because Tristan was an angel we could fly"—Gregory got up and started pacing around the bedroom—"but we couldn't, and we fell off the top of this high fence."

Ivy glanced down at her brother's wrapped ankle. His knees were cut and bruised.

"Then we heard the train whistle. And we had to keep going. When we got closer we saw you on the platform. We shouted to you, Ivy, but you didn't hear us. We ran up the steps and over the bridge. That's when we saw the other Tristan. The one in the cap and jacket, just like in your picture," he said, pointing to it.

Ivy shivered.

"So," Gregory said, "angel Tristan is in two places now—with you, and on the other side of the tracks as well. He's playing a trick on Ivy, calling her over to him. It wasn't a very nice trick."

"Tristan was with me," Philip said.

"Then who was across the tracks?" Gregory asked.

"A bad angel," Philip replied with complete certainty. "Someone who wanted Ivy to die."

Gregory blinked.

Ivy sank back against her headboard. As bizarre as Philip's story sounded, it seemed more real to her than the idea that she had taken drugs and thrown herself in front of a train. And the fact remained that somehow her brother had gotten there and he had pulled her back at the last moment. The engineer had seen the blur in front of his train and radioed in that he could not stop in time.

"I thought you saw Tristan," Philip said.

"What?" Ivy asked.

"You turned around. I thought you saw his light." Philip gazed at her hopefully.

Ivy shook her head. "I don't remember it. I don't remember anything from the train station."

Perhaps it would be easier if she never recalled what had happened, Ivy thought. But every time she looked at the photo now, there was a prickling in the back of her mind. Something wouldn't let her look away and forget. Ivy stared until the picture ran blurry. She didn't realize she had begun to cry.

"Ivy . . . Ivy, don't."

Suzanne's words jolted Ivy back into the present. As she lifted her head her friend crouched down next to the school locker. Her mouth was a grim, lipsticked line. Beth, who had also come back from orientation, stood above her, fumbling through her knapsack for tissues. She glanced down at Ivy, her own brimming eyes reflecting Ivy's tears.

"I'm okay," Ivy said, wiping her eyes quickly,

looking from one to the other. "Really, I'm okay."

But she could tell they didn't believe her. Gregory had driven her to school that day, and Suzanne would be taking her home. It was as if they didn't trust her to drive herself, as if they thought that at any minute she'd lose it and steer right off a cliff.

"You shouldn't have that picture taped inside your locker," Suzanne said. "Sooner or later you're going to have to let go, Ivy. You're just making yourself—" She hesitated.

"Crazy?"

Suzanne smoothed back her mane of black hair, then toyed with a gold hoop earring. She had never been shy about speaking her mind before, but now she was being careful. "It's not healthy, Ivy," she said at last. "It's not good to have his picture here to remind you every time you open the door."

"But I wasn't the one who put it here," Ivy told her.

Suzanne frowned. "What do you mean?"

"Did you see me do it?" Ivy asked.

"Well, no, but you've got to remember—" her friend began.

"I don't."

Suzanne and Beth exchanged glances.

"So someone else must have," Ivy said, sounding a lot more certain than she was. "It's a school picture. Anyone could get a copy of it. I didn't tape it here, so someone else must have."

There was a moment of silence. Suzanne sighed.

"Did you see the counselor today?" Beth asked.

"I just came from there," Ivy told her, closing her locker, leaving the picture inside. She stood up next to Beth, whose outfit had also been selected by Suzanne. But Beth, no matter how fashionably dressed, would always look to Ivy like a wide-eyed owl, with her round face and feathers of frosted hair.

"What did Ms. Bryce say?" Beth asked as they started down the hall.

"Nothing much. I'm supposed to come talk to her twice a week and check in if I'm having a bad day. So you're both coming Monday?" Ivy asked, changing the subject.

Suzanne's eyes brightened. "To the Baines Bash? It's a Labor Day tradition!" She sounded relieved to be talking about a party.

Ivy knew that the last month had been hard on Suzanne. She'd been so jealous of the attention Gregory paid Ivy that she'd stopped speaking to her oldest friend. Later, when Gregory told Suzanne that Ivy had tried to commit suicide, she blamed herself for turning her back. But Ivy knew that she herself was partly to blame for the rift. She'd gotten too close to Gregory. In the three weeks since the incident at the train station, Gregory had cooled toward Ivy, treating her more like a sister than a girl he was romantically interested in. Suzanne had reached out to Ivy again, and Ivy was glad for the change in both of them.

"We've been going to the Baines Bash since we were kids," Beth told Ivy. "Everybody in Stonehill has."

"Except me," Ivy pointed out.

"And Will. He moved here last winter, like you," Beth said. "I told him about the party, and he's coming."

"Is he?" Ivy had noticed that Beth and Will were hanging around together more and more. "He's a nice guy."

"Real nice," Beth said enthusiastically.

They studied each other for a moment. Were Beth and Will getting to be more than friends? Ivy wondered. After writing all those romantic stories, maybe Beth had finally fallen. It wouldn't be hard to do: A lot of girls had crushes on Will. Ivy herself found that whenever she looked into his dark brown eyes— She caught herself and quickly shoved aside that thought. She would never let herself fall in love again.

The girls pushed through the school doors, and Suzanne led them on a roundabout route to their cars that conveniently ran past the field where the football team was practicing.

"I have to get a team program," Suzanne said after several minutes of watching. "What if I start drooling over number forty-nine and discover he's just a sophomore?"

"A hunk's a hunk," Beth replied philosophically. "And older women with younger guys are in."

"Don't tell Gregory I'm looking," Suzanne said in a stage whisper as they moved on toward their cars.

"Isn't looking allowed?" Beth asked innocently.

"On second thought, tell him, tell him!" Suzanne

said, flinging her arms out dramatically. "Let him know, Ivy, I'm out and looking."

Ivy just smiled. From the beginning, Suzanne and Gregory had played mind games with each other.

"I mean, why should I tie myself down to one guy?" Suzanne continued.

Ivy knew this was just an act. Suzanne had been obsessed with Gregory since March and wanted desperately to tie him down to her.

"I'm going to start at the Baines Bash." She unlocked her car door. "That's where a lot of school romances have started, you know."

"How many are you planning for yourself?" Ivy teased.

"Six."

"Great," Beth said. "That's six more heartbreaks for me to write about."

"I'd settle for five romances," Suzanne added, giving Ivy a sly look, "if you'll take the other one and stop thinking about Tristan."

Ivy didn't reply.

Suzanne got in her car, closed the door, and reached across to unlock the passenger-side door. But before Ivy could open it, Beth caught her hand. She spoke quickly, quietly: "You can't forget, Ivy. Not yet. It would be dangerous to forget."

In the back of her mind, Ivy felt that prickling feeling again.

Then Beth yanked open her own car door, hopped in, and drove away fast.

Suzanne glanced in the rearview mirror, frowning. "I don't know what's gotten into that girl. Lately she's been hopping around like a scared rabbit. What did she just say to you?"

Ivy shrugged. "Just gave me a little advice."

"Don't tell me—she got another one of her premonitions."

Ivy remained silent.

Suzanne laughed. "You've got to admit, Ivy, Beth's flaky. I never take her 'advice' seriously. You shouldn't, either."

"I haven't so far," Ivy said. And both times, she thought, I've been sorry I didn't.

2

"Yo! Romeo! Where art thou? Rooo-me-ooo," Lacey called.

Tristan, who had been following Ivy down the wide center stair of the Baines home, stopped at the landing and stuck his head out an open window.

Lacey smiled up at him from the middle of a flower bed, the only piece of Andrew Baines's property that hadn't been overrun by the hundreds of guests with their picnic blankets and baskets. A Caribbean steel band was warming up on the patio. Paper lanterns hung from the pines around the tennis court; beneath them tables were laid out with refreshments.

Long before Tristan met Ivy, long before Andrew surprised everyone by marrying Maggie, Tristan had come to this annual party. He remembered how huge the white clapboard home had seemed to him as a little boy, with its east and west wings and double chimneys and rows of heavy black shutters—like a house that would be pictured in his mother's New England calendar.

"Ditch the chick, Romeo," Lacey called up to him. "You're missing a great party. Especially under some of the bushes."

Even now, after two and a half months of being an angel, Tristan's first instinct was to quiet her. But no one else could hear them, except when Lacey chose to project her voice, a power he hadn't yet mastered. He gave her a lopsided smile, then withdrew from the window. At the same moment that Tristan turned back toward the stairs, Ivy stopped and turned toward the window.

Instantly he began hoping. She senses something, he thought.

But Ivy looked right through him, then without hesitation moved past him. She leaned upon the sill of the window, gazing wistfully at the scene before her. Tristan stood beside her and watched as torches were lit, flaring up suddenly in the summer twilight.

Ivy turned her head, and Tristan did, too, following her gaze to Will, who was standing at the edge of the crowd, surveying it. Suddenly Will looked up, meeting Ivy's eyes. Tristan knew what Will saw: brilliant green eyes and a tumbleweed of blond hair falling over her shoulders.

Ivy looked down at Will for what seemed like forever, then stepped back abruptly, her hands going up to her cheeks. Tristan pulled back just as fast. Take a picture, Will, it lasts longer, he thought, then quickly descended the steps.

Lacey was waiting on the patio, amusing herself by hitting the drummer's cymbal every time he turned his back. Of course, the drummer didn't see her, not even the purple shimmer that some believers glimpsed. She winked at Tristan.

"I'm not here to fool around," he said.

"Okay, sweetie, let's get down to business," Lacey said, giving him a little push. Though they could slip through other people's bodies, they appeared and felt solid to each other.

"I want to show you someone who's gulping down drinks over by the tennis court," Lacey told him, but first she headed for Philip's tree house. She simply couldn't resist the opportunity to knock away the tree's swing seat when a girl in a pink sundress tried to sit on it.

"Lacey, act your age."

"I will," she said, "just as soon as you decide to act like an angel."

"Seems to me I am," he said.

She shook her head. Her purple spiked hair, like his own thick brown crop, did not move with the breeze. "Repeat after me," Lacey instructed in an obnoxious teacher voice. "Ivy's breathing, Will's breathing, *I'm not.*"

"It's just that she looked straight at me at the train station," Tristan said. "I was sure she believed again. When I pulled her and Philip back, I was sure Ivy saw me."

"If she did, she's forgotten it," Lacey said.

"I have to get her to remember. Beth—"

"Is feeling too rattled to help you out," Lacey cut in. "She predicted the break-in, then foresaw danger that night at the train station. She has a special gift, but she's too frightened to be an open channel anymore."

"Then Philip."

"Philip! Oh, *puh-lease*. How long do you think Gregory's going to put up with the kid who keeps talking about angel Tristan?"

Tristan knew she was right.

"That leaves Will," Lacey said. She walked backward and pointed a long purple nail at him. "So. Just how jealous are you?"

"Very," he replied honestly, then sighed. "You know how you feel about the actress who took your place in that film, the one you said stinks?"

"She *does* stink," Lacey said quickly.

"Multiply that feeling by a thousand. And the thing is, Will's not a bad guy. He'd be good for Ivy, and all I want is what's good for Ivy. I love her. I'd do anything for her—"

"Die, for instance," Lacey said. "But you've already tried that, and look where it got you."

Tristan grimaced. "Time with you."

She grinned, then nudged him. "Look over there. Next to the lady who looks like she got her perm and cut at the poodle parlor. Recognize him?"

"It's Caroline's friend," Tristan said, observing the tall dark-haired man. "The one who leaves roses on her grave."

"He creamed Andrew at tennis and looked like he enjoyed every minute of it."

"Did you find out his name?" Tristan asked.

"Tom Stetson. He's a teacher at Andrew's college. I tell you, who needs soap operas when you can hang around Stonehill? Do you think it was a long, torrid, secret affair? Do you think Andrew knew? Yo, Tristan!"

"I hear you," he said, but his eyes were focused on the crowd twenty feet away, where Ivy, Will, and Beth were talking.

"*Oh,* the *arrows* of *love,*" Lacey crooned. He hated it when she exaggerated her words like that. "I swear, Tristan, that girl's put so many holes in you, one day you're going to fold over like a slice of Swiss cheese."

He grimaced.

"It's pathetic, the way you look at her with those big puppy dog eyes. She doesn't even see you. I just hope that one day—"

"Know what I hope, Lacey?" Tristan asked, swinging around to her. "I hope you fall in love."

Lacey blinked with surprise.

"I hope you fall in love with a guy who looks right past you."

Lacey looked away.

"And I hope you do it soon, before I finish my

mission," Tristan went on. "I want to be around to make lots of jokes about it."

He expected Lacey to make a snappy comeback, but she kept her eyes away from him, watching Ivy's cat, Ella, who had followed them through the crowd.

"I can't wait till the day," Tristan continued, "that Lacey Lovitt falls in love with some guy beyond her reach."

"What makes you think I haven't?" she muttered, then crouched down to scratch Ella. She petted the cat for several minutes.

After two years of procrastinating on her own mission, Lacey had developed more endurance and more powers than Tristan. He knew that she could keep the tips of her fingers materialized to scratch the cat much longer than he.

"Come on, Ella," Lacey said softly, and Tristan saw the cat's ears prick. Lacey was projecting her voice.

Ella followed Lacey, and Tristan followed Ella to a refreshment table. Eric and Gregory were standing there. Eric was arguing with Gregory and the bartender, trying to convince them to give him a beer.

Lacey gave Ella a nudge, and the cat leaped up lightly on the table. The three guys didn't notice her.

"A bowl of milk, please."

"Just a minute, miss," the bartender said, turning away from Gregory and Eric. His eyes widened as they fell upon Ella.

Ella winked.

The bartender turned back to the boys. "Did you hear that?"

"Milk, and hurry it up, please."

Now Eric and the bartender stared at the cat. Gregory craned his neck to glance behind Eric. "What's the problem?" he said impatiently. "Just fix an iced tea."

"I prefer milk."

The bartender lowered his face to Ella's. She meowed at him and leaped down from the table. Lacey snickered, but she had stopped projecting her voice, and only Tristan could hear her now.

The bartender, his brow still furrowed, poured the iced tea for Eric. Then Gregory flicked his head to the right, and he and Eric started off in that direction. Tristan trailed them as they wove their way through the crowd and beyond it, to the stone wall that marked the edge of the property.

Far below them was the tiny train station and the track that hugged the river. Even Tristan could hardly believe that he and Philip had made it down this side of the ridge. It was steep and rocky, with little to cling to but narrow stone ledges and an occasional shrub or dwarfed tree.

"No way," Gregory muttered to himself. "That kid's lying to me, covering up. Who's in with him?"

"Just let me know when you're talking to me," Eric said cheerfully.

Gregory glanced at him.

"You've been doing it a lot lately, talking to

yourself"—Eric grinned—"or maybe to the angels."

"Screw the angels," Gregory said.

Eric laughed. "Yeah, well, maybe you should start praying to them. You've gotten yourself in deep, Gregory." His face grew serious, his eyes narrowing. "Real deep. And you're getting me in with you."

"You idiot! You're getting yourself in. You're always high—and you're always messing up. I'm asking you one more time, where're the clothes?"

"I'm telling you one more time, I don't have them."

"I want the cap and the jacket," Gregory said. "And you're going to find them for me, because if you don't, Jimmy's not getting the money you owe." Gregory tilted back his head. "And you know what that means. You know how touchy those dealers can be when they don't get their money."

Eric's mouth twitched. Without alcohol he could not stand up to Gregory. "I'm sick of it," he whined. "I'm sick of doing your dirty work."

He started to walk away, but Gregory yanked him back by the arm. "But you'll do it, won't you? And you'll keep quiet about things, because you need me. You need your fix."

Eric struggled weakly. "Let me go. Someone's watching."

Gregory loosened his grip and looked around. Eric quickly stepped out of his reach. "Be careful, Gregory," he warned. "I can feel them watching."

Gregory arched his eyebrows and began to laugh

menacingly. Even when Eric was out of sight, he continued to chuckle.

Lacey wriggled her shoulders. "Major creepo," she said.

They watched as Gregory worked his way back into the party, talking and smiling at the guests.

"What do you think Eric's dirty work was?" Lacey asked Tristan. "Knocking off Caroline? Cutting your brake line? Attacking Ivy in Andrew's office?" She materialized her fingers and hurled a stone as far as she could over the ridge. "Of course, we don't even know for sure if Caroline was murdered or if your brake line was deliberately cut."

Tristan nodded. "I'm going to have to time-travel through Eric's memories again."

Lacey had picked up another stone and now dropped it to her side. "You're going back through Eric's mind? You're crazy, Tristan! I thought you learned your lesson the first time. His circuits are fried, it's too dangerous, and his memories won't give you any proof."

"Once I know what is going on, I can find the proof," he reasoned.

Lacey shook her head.

"Right now," Tristan said, "I've got to get Ivy to remember what happened at the train station. I've got to find Will and convince him to help me."

"Gee, what a great idea," Lacey said. "I think someone else suggested that about fifteen minutes ago."

Tristan shrugged.

"That same someone will come with you, in case you need further help," she added.

"No jokes, Lacey," he warned.

"No promises, Tristan."

They found Will by the patio, dancing with Beth. Ivy and Suzanne were sitting next to Ivy's mother, watching kids from their class getting into the reggae music. Lacey started dancing by herself, swinging her hips, lifting her hands above her head, then dropping them to her waist. She's good at it, Tristan observed as she twisted and turned her way across the patio. Ella, seeing Lacey's light, began to follow her. Somebody stepped backward and fell over Ella, landing on his rear next to the cat.

"Would you like to dance?" It was Lacey's projected voice.

The guy stared at Ella for a moment, then scrambled to his feet.

"Come here, Ella," Maggie called out, and the cat sauntered toward Ivy's mother, with Lacey following. Ella leaped into Maggie's lap, and Ivy's mother settled back to watch the dancers.

"No one will ask me to dance, Maggie." Lacey again.

Maggie shifted the cat around, cupping Ella's chin in her perfectly manicured hand, staring at the cat as if she expected her to speak once more.

"Did you girls hear that?" Maggie asked, but neither replied. Suzanne was giving Ivy a detailed analysis of the relationships of all the couples on the patio.

24

Tristan left Lacey to her games and moved through the crowd toward Beth and Will. They were dancing with their heads as close as a romantic couple's, but he knew why Beth and Will were really together—Ivy.

"I'm afraid," Beth said. "I know things I don't want to know—I know them before they happen, Will. And I write things I never meant to write."

"I draw pictures I never meant to draw," Will replied.

"I wish someone would tell us what's going on. Whatever it is, it's not over yet—that much I know. I have this sense that things are terribly wrong, and they're going to get worse. I wake up scared, scared to death for Ivy. Sometimes I think I'm cracking up."

Will drew her closer. Tristan glanced over at Ivy and saw her quickly turn her head away.

"You're not cracking up, Beth. It's just that you have some kind of gift that—"

"I don't want this kind of gift!" she cried.

"Shhh. Shhh." With his hand, he smoothed Beth's hair.

"She's watching us," Beth said. "She'll get the wrong idea. You'd better ask her to dance."

Tristan knew at that moment what Will would be thinking. He gazed at Ivy and thought how it would feel to put his arms around her, to pull her to him, to let his fingers get lost in her bright hair. In that instant they matched thoughts, and Tristan slipped inside Will.

Will suddenly sagged against Beth. "It's that feeling again. I hate the feeling."

"I need to talk to Ivy," Tristan told him, and Will spoke the words aloud.

"What are you going to say to her?" Beth asked.

Will shook his head, bewildered.

"Ask Ivy to dance," Tristan said, and once again Will spoke the words as if they were his own.

"You ask her," Beth replied.

Will's jaw tightened. Tristan could feel his struggle, how Will's instinct told him to thrust the intruder out of his mind, and how his curiosity fought back against this instinct. "Who are you?" Will wondered silently.

"It's Tristan. Tristan. You've got to believe me now."

"I can't believe," Beth said.

Will and she had stopped dancing and stood looking at each other, trying to understand.

"He's inside you, isn't he?" Beth asked, her voice shaking.

"It's his words you're saying."

Will nodded.

"Can you make him leave?" she asked.

"Don't!"

"Why don't you leave us alone?" Beth cried.

"I can't. For Ivy's sake, I can't."

Will and Beth clung to each other. Then Will led her to the edge of the patio, where Ivy was sitting. "Will you dance with me?" he asked Ivy.

She glanced at Beth uncertainly.

"I'm beat," Beth said, pulling Ivy up out of the chair and taking her place. "Go on. I've got to give these dainty, size-nine feet a break."

Will walked quietly with Ivy to the least crowded part of the patio. Tristan felt him tremble as he put his arms around her. He felt each awkward step and remembered how he himself had felt the previous spring when he had first tried to get to know Ivy. Face-to-face with her, he couldn't manage a sentence with more than four words.

"How are you?" Will asked.

"Fine."

"Good."

A long silence followed. Tristan could feel questions forming in Will's mind. "If you're there," Will said silently to Tristan, "why aren't you telling me what to do?"

"I'm not that fragile," Ivy told him.

"What?"

"You're dancing with me as if you think I'll break," she said loudly, her green eyes shooting brilliant sparks.

Will looked at her, surprised. "You're angry."

"You noticed," she said sharply. "I'm tired of the way people are acting—everyone's being so careful around me! Tiptoeing, as though they're afraid they'll do something to set me off. Well, I've got news for you, Will, and everyone else. I'm not made of glass, and I'm not about to shatter. Got it?"

"I think so," Will said. Then, without warning,

he spun her around twice, pushing her away from him and drawing her back like a yo-yo. He dropped his arm so she fell back, then he caught her at the last instant, leaning over her and pulling her up.

"Is that better?"

Ivy pushed back the hair that had tumbled over her face, and she laughed breathlessly. "A little."

Will grinned. Both of them were more relaxed now—it was time to speak to her, Tristan thought. But what could he say that wouldn't anger her again or scare her away?

"There's something I want to talk about," Will said, using Tristan's words.

Ivy pulled back a little to look into his eyes, then quickly glanced away. Eyes a girl could drown in—that was how Lacey had described Will's. And that's why Ivy looked away, Tristan thought, struggling to control his jealousy.

"It's about . . . Beth. She's kind of shaken up," Will said for Tristan. "You know how she has premonitions."

"I know I gave her a good scare a few weeks ago," Ivy said, "but that was just a—"

Will shook his head quickly, as Tristan did. "Beth is more afraid of the future than of what happened then."

"What do you mean?" Ivy asked. Her tone was indignant, but Tristan heard the slight tremor. "Nothing more is going to happen," she insisted. "What do I have to do to convince everyone that I'm okay?"

"You have to remember, Ivy."

"Remember what?" she asked.

"The night of the accident."

Tristan could feel Will pulling back now, wondering what his words were leading to. "What accident?" Will asked silently. "The one you died in?"

"The accident?" Ivy repeated. "Is that a nice, polite way of talking about my attempted suicide?"

"Ivy, you can't believe that! You know it's not true," Will said, passionately speaking each word Tristan gave him.

"I don't know anything anymore," she replied, her voice breaking.

"Try to remember," Will pleaded for Tristan. "You saw me at the train station."

"You were there?" she asked with surprise.

"I've always been there for you. I love you!"

Ivy stared at Will. Too late Tristan realized his mistake in speaking directly.

"You can't, Will."

Will swallowed hard.

"You should love someone else. I—I'll never love you."

Tristan felt Will take the blow.

"I'll never love anyone again," Ivy said, stepping back, "not the way I loved Tristan."

"Tell her it's me speaking," Tristan urged.

But Will stood still and said nothing. Other couples bumped into them, laughed, and danced around them. Will held Ivy at arm's length, and Ivy would not meet his gaze. She turned suddenly, and Will let her walk away.

"Go after her," Tristan ordered. "We're not finished."

"Leave me alone," Will muttered, and started off in the other direction, his head down.

Gregory, who was leading Suzanne into the crowd of dancers, caught Will by the arm. "You're not giving up, are you?"

"Giving up?" Will repeated, his voice sounding hollow.

"On Ivy," Suzanne said.

"On the chase," Gregory said, grinning at Will.

"I don't think Ivy wants to be chased."

"Oh, come on," Gregory chided him. "My sweet and innocent stepsister loves to play games. And take it from me, she's a pro."

A pro at escaping you, Tristan thought as he moved out of Will.

"I'd never give up," Gregory said, glancing at Ivy, who was standing at the edge of the patio. His lingering smile made both Suzanne and Tristan turn toward Ivy uneasily. "There's nothing I like more than a girl who plays hard to get."

3

"Therefore," Philip told Ivy on Wednesday evening, "I can watch *Jurassic Park* again."

"Therefore?" Ivy repeated with a smile. Leaning over her mother's hand, she quickly repainted Maggie's nails. Her mother and Andrew were headed for another college fund-raiser.

"Andrew said so."

"So he's already checked your homework?" Ivy asked.

"He said my story about the party was highly imaginative and very fine."

"Highly imaginative and very fine," Maggie mimicked. "Before you know it, we're going to have a four-foot-tall professor walking around here."

Ivy smiled again. "Go set up the VCR," she told Philip. "As soon as Mom and I are finished, I'll be down."

She lifted the scarlet brush just in time as Philip jumped off the bed, leaving her and her mother bouncing.

When he was outside the door, Maggie whispered to Ivy, "Gregory said he'd stay around tonight, so if Philip gives you any trouble—"

Ivy frowned. She had always been able to handle Philip much better than either her mother or Gregory could.

"—or if you start to feel, you know, under the weather . . ."

Ivy knew what her mother meant—depressed, crazy, suicidal. Maggie couldn't bring herself to say those words, but she had accepted what others told her about Ivy. There was no fighting it, so Ivy just ignored it. "It's nice of Andrew to help with Philip's schoolwork," she said.

"Andrew cares about both you and Philip," her mother replied. "I've been wanting to discuss this with you, Ivy, but with everything so, well, you know, in the last three weeks . . ."

"Spit it out, Mom."

"Andrew has filed adoption papers."

Ivy blobbed Scarlet Passion on her mother's knuckle. "You're kidding."

"We're going ahead with it for Philip," her mother said, wiping the knuckle off. "But you'll be eighteen soon. It's up to you to decide what you'd like to do."

Ivy didn't know what to say. She wondered if

Gregory knew about this, and if he did, what he thought about it. Now his father would have two sons, and it was becoming more and more obvious that Andrew preferred Philip.

"Andrew wants you to know that you will always have a home here. We love you very much, Ivy. No one could love you more." Her mother spoke quickly and nervously. "Day by day, it's going to get better for you. It really will, honey. People fall in love more than once," Maggie went on, talking faster and faster. "Someday you'll meet someone special. You'll be happy again. Please believe me," she pleaded.

Ivy capped the bottle of polish. When she stood up, her mother remained sitting on the bed, looking up at Ivy with a concerned expression, her red fingernails spread out on her lap. Ivy leaned down and kissed her mother gently on the forehead, where all the lines of worry were. "It's already getting better," she said. "Come on, let me blast those beauties with the hair dryer."

After Maggie and Andrew left, Ivy settled down on the couch in the family room to watch *Jurassic Park*'s dinosaurs thump and thrash. She stuck a pillow behind her head and propped her feet up on the stool that her brother was leaning against. Ella jumped up and stretched out on Ivy's long legs, resting a furry chin on Ivy's knee.

Ivy petted the cat absentmindedly. Tired from her nonstop performance over the last few days, her cheerful effort to prove to everyone that she was okay, she felt her eyelids getting heavy. With the first tremors from the storm at Jurassic Park, Ivy was asleep.

Scenes from school ran together in a constantly shifting dream, with Ms. Bryce's pie face, her probing little counselor eyes, fading in and out. Ivy was in the classroom, then the school halls—walking down endless school halls. Teachers and kids were lined up on the sides watching her.

"I'm okay. I'm happy. I'm okay. I'm happy," she said over and over.

Outside the school, a storm was brewing. She could hear it through the walls, she could feel the walls shaking. Now she could see it, the fresh green leaves of May being torn off the trees, branches whipping back and forth against the inky sky.

She was driving now, not walking. The wind rocked her car, and lightning split the sky. She knew she was lost. A feeling of dread began to grow in her. She didn't know where she was going, yet the dread grew as if she were getting closer and closer to something terrible. Suddenly a red Harley came around the bend. The motorcyclist slowed down. For a moment she thought he'd stop to help her, but he sped by. She drove around the bend in the road and saw the window.

She knew that window, the great glass rectangle with a dark shadow behind it. The car picked up speed. She was rushing toward the window. She tried to stop, tried to brake, pressed the pedal down again and again, but the car would not stop. It would not slow down! Then the door opened, and Ivy rolled out. She staggered. She could hardly hold herself up. She thought she'd fall into the great glass window.

A train whistle sounded, long and piercing. A dark shadow loomed larger and larger behind the glass. Ivy reached out with one hand. The glass exploded—a train burst through it. For a moment time froze, the flying glass hanging in the air like icicles, the huge train motionless, pausing before it slammed her to her death.

Then hands pulled her back. The train rushed by, and the shards of glass melted into the ground. The storm had passed, though it was still dark—the kind of sky one sees just before dawn. Ivy wondered whose hands had pulled her back; they were as strong as an angel's. Looking down, she found she was holding on to Philip.

She marveled at the peacefulness surrounding them now. Perhaps it really was dawn—she saw a faint glimmer of light. The light grew stronger. It became as long as a person, and its edges shimmered with colors. It wasn't the sun, though it warmed her heart to see it. It circled Philip and her, coming closer and closer.

"Who's there?" Ivy asked. "Who's there?" She wasn't afraid. For the first time in a long while, she felt full of hope. "Who's there?" she cried out, wanting to hold on to that hope.

"Gregory." He shook her awake. He rocked Ivy hard. "It's Gregory!"

He was sitting next to her on the couch, gripping her arms. Philip stood by her other side, clutching the VCR remote.

"You were dreaming again," Gregory said. His body was tense. His eyes searched hers. "I thought the dreams were over. It's been three weeks—I was hoping. . . ."

Ivy shut her eyes for a moment. She wanted to see the light, the shimmering again. She wanted to get away from Gregory and back to the feeling of a powerful hope. His words ate away at the edges of it.

"What?" he asked her. "What is it, Ivy?"

She didn't answer him.

"Talk to me!" he said. "Please." His voice had softened to a plea. "Why are you looking that way? Was there something new in the dream?"

"No." She saw the doubt in his eyes. "Just at the beginning," she added quickly. "Before I was driving through the storm, I was walking down the halls at school, and everyone was staring at me."

"Staring," he repeated. "That's all?"

She nodded.

"I guess it's been hard for you the last few days," Gregory said, gently touching her cheek with his finger.

Ivy wished he would leave her alone. With each moment she spent near him, the dream's light and its feeling of hope faded.

"I know it's hard facing all the gossip at school," Gregory added, his voice full of sympathy.

Ivy didn't want to hear it. If she could find hope again, she didn't need his or anybody's sympathy. She closed her eyes, wishing she could block him out, but she could feel him staring at her, just like the others.

"I'm surprised your, uh, experience at the train station wasn't part of your dream," he said.

"Me too," she replied, opening her eyes, wondering if he knew she was holding back. "I'm fine, Gregory, really. Go back to whatever you were doing."

Ivy couldn't explain why she held back, except that the light seemed to be growing weaker and weaker in Gregory's presence.

"I was fixing a snack," he said. "You want anything?"

"No, thanks."

Gregory nodded and left the room, still looking concerned. Ivy waited till she heard him banging around in the kitchen, then dropped down on the floor next to her brother, who was watching the movie again.

"Philip," she said softly, "the night at the train station, after you saved me, was there some kind of shimmering light?"

Philip turned to her, his eyes wide. "You're remembering!"

"Shhh." Ivy glanced in the direction of the kitchen, listening to Gregory's movements. Then she sat back against the stool and tried to sort out the images in her mind. She saw the light from her dream as if it were in the train station, on the platform, not far from Philip and her. Had she made that up, or was she finally remembering?

"What did the light do?" she asked her brother. "Did it move?"

Philip thought for a moment. "He was walking around us, like in a circle."

"That's how it was in my dream," Ivy said. Then she turned her head and quickly put her finger to her lips.

When Gregory entered a minute later, Philip and she were sitting side by side, watching the movie intently.

"I thought some tea might help you calm down," Gregory said, crouching down next to her, handing her a warm mug. He handed Philip a Yoo-hoo.

"Hey, thanks," Philip said happily.

Gregory nodded and glanced back at Ivy. "Don't you want it?"

"Uh, sure. I-it's fine—great," she stammered, surprised by the double image that had just flashed before her eyes: Gregory as he was now and Gregory standing in her bedroom. When she took the drink from Gregory's hands, she saw him handing her another cup of steaming tea. Then she saw him as if he were sitting close to her, sitting on her bed and holding the cup to her lips, urging her to drink.

"Would you rather have something else?" Gregory asked.

"No, this is fine." Was she remembering that

night? Could Gregory have given her drugged tea?

"You look pale," he said, and touched her bare arm. "You're ice cold, Ivy."

Her arm was covered with goose bumps. He ran his hand up and down it. Ivy became aware of just how strong his fingers were. Gregory had held her many times since Tristan's death, but for the first time Ivy noticed the power in his grip. He was staring beyond her now, at the television screen, at a person getting thrashed by a dinosaur.

"Gregory, you're hurting my arm."

He released her quickly and sat back on his heels to look at her. It was impossible to read the thoughts behind his light gray eyes.

"You still seem upset," he observed.

"Just tired," Ivy replied. "I'm tired of people watching me, waiting for . . . for I don't know what."

"Waiting for you to crack up?" he suggested softly.

"I guess so," she said. But I won't, she thought. And I haven't yet, despite what you or anyone thinks.

"Thanks for the tea," she said. "I'm feeling better. I think I'll sit awhile with Philip and watch these guys become dinosaur munchies."

One side of Gregory's mouth drew up a little.

"Thanks," Ivy repeated. "I don't know what I'd do without you."

He rested his hand on top of hers for a moment, then left her and Philip to watch the video. As soon as Ivy heard him climb the steps, she poured her tea into a potted plant. Philip was too engrossed in the film to notice.

Ivy sat back on the sofa and closed her eyes, trying to remember what the light was like, trying to hold on to the glimmer of hope her dream had given her.

Could it be true? Had Philip been seeing him all along? Was an angel there for her? Her eyes tingled with tears. Was it Tristan?

"Tristan?" Ivy called softly, and shivered with excitement. She had hidden in the school locker room Thursday afternoon, waiting till the swimming pool was empty and the coach had left for a faculty meeting. Then, fully dressed, she had slipped off her shoes and climbed the thin silver ladder. Now she stood on the board high above the pool, just as she had the previous April.

Though Ivy could swim now, some of the old fear remained. She took three steps forward and felt the board flex beneath her. Gritting her teeth, Ivy stared down at the aqua water, streaked and spangled by the fluorescent lights. She would never love the water the way Tristan had, but this was where he had first reached out to her. This was where she had to try to reach back to him.

"Tristan?" she called softly.

The only sound was the steady buzzing of the fluorescent lights.

Angels, help me! Help me reach him.

Ivy didn't say the words out loud. After Tristan's death, she had stopped praying to her angels. After losing him, she couldn't find the words; she couldn't believe they would be heard. But this prayer felt as if it were burning its way out of her heart.

She took two more steps forward. "Tristan!" she cried out loud. "Are you there?"

She walked to the end of board and stood with her toes at the very edge. "Tristan, where are you?" Her voice echoed back from the concrete walls. "I love you!" she cried. "I love you!"

Ivy dropped her head. He wasn't there. He couldn't hear her. She should get down before someone caught her up there, acting crazy.

Ivy took a step back from the edge. Watching her feet, she slowly and carefully turned around on the board. When she looked up, she gasped.

At the other end of the board, the air shimmered. It was like liquid light—a gold stem burning in the rough shape of a person. The glowing shape was surrounded by a mist of sheer and trembling colors. This was what she had seen at the train station.

"Tristan," she said softly. She reached out her hand and started walking toward him. She longed to be enveloped by his golden light, surrounded by the colors, embraced by all that Tristan was now.

"Tell me it's you. Speak to me," she begged. "Tristan!"

"Ivy!"

"Ivy!"

The two voices slammed off the walls—Gregory's and Suzanne's.

"Ivy, what are you doing up there?"

"She's cracking up, Gregory! I was afraid this would happen."

Ivy looked down and saw Gregory already two steps up the ladder and Suzanne looking about frantically. "I'll get help," Suzanne said. "I'll go get Ms. Bryce."

"Wait," Gregory said.

"But, Gregory, she's—"

"Wait." It was a command. Suzanne fell silent.

"There are enough stories about Ivy going around already. We can handle her ourselves."

Handle her? Ivy repeated silently. They were talking about her as if she were a mischievous child or maybe a crazy girl who couldn't take care of herself.

"I'll get her down," Gregory said calmly.

"I'll get myself down," Ivy said. "If I need any help, Tristan is here."

"I told you—she's gone, Gregory! Totally nuts! Don't you see—"

"Suzanne," Ivy shouted down at her, "can't you see his light?"

Now Gregory was scrambling up the ladder.

"There's nothing there, Ivy. Nothing," Suzanne moaned.

"Look," Ivy said, and pointed. "Right there!" Then she stared across the board at Gregory, who had pulled himself up on it. Suzanne was right. There was nothing there, no shimmering colors, no golden light.

"Tristan?"

"Gregory," he said in a hoarse whisper, then he held out his hand.

Ivy looked to either side of her. Was she going crazy? Had she had imagined it all? "Tristan?"

"That's enough, Ivy. Come down now."

She didn't want to go with him. She longed to go back to the golden light, to be surrounded by it again. She'd give anything to be held inside that moment with Tristan.

"Come here, Ivy. Don't make this difficult."

Ivy hated his patronizing tone.

"Come on!" Gregory ordered. "Do you want me to get Ms. Bryce?"

She glared at him, but she knew she couldn't fight him. "No," Ivy said at last. "I can get down by myself. Go ahead. Go ahead! I'll follow you."

"Good girl," Gregory said, then descended the ladder. Ivy walked to the end of the board and turned around. She was about to back down the first step when Suzanne called out. "Will! Over here! Hurry."

"Be quiet, Suzanne," Gregory said.

But Will, who had just come into the pool area, saw Ivy up on the board and ran toward Gregory and Suzanne. "Beth said you were looking for her," he said to them breathlessly. "Is she okay? What was she trying to do?"

The resentment burning in Ivy now flared into anger.

She. Her. They were talking about her as if she couldn't hear them, as if she couldn't understand.

"She and her are right here!" Ivy shouted down at them. "You don't have to talk about me as though my mind has gone."

"She thinks Tristan's up there and is going to help her," Suzanne told Will. "She said something about Tristan's light."

With that, Will gazed up at Ivy. Ivy glared down at him. Her furious stare was met with a look of wonder. His eyes traveled along the board behind her, searching. He glanced quickly around the pool, then up at her again. She saw the word "Tristan" on his lips, though he did not speak it aloud. At last he asked her, "Can you get down all right?"

"Of course I can."

Gregory and Suzanne stood on either side of the ladder as she climbed down, as if they might have to catch her. Will stood apart from them and continued to glance around the pool.

When Ivy reached the bottom, Suzanne hugged her, then held her at arm's length. "Girl, I could just shake you, shake you." She was laughing, but Ivy saw the tears in her friend's eyes and the relief in her face.

Gregory stepped in then and put his arms around Ivy, pulling her close. "You scared me, Ivy," he said. Ivy could barely breathe and tried to pull back, but he wouldn't let go.

Suzanne laid a hand on Gregory's arm. She was over her scare now and did not look happy about the long embrace. Will kept his distance, saying nothing.

"I'll take you home," Gregory said, freeing Ivy at last.

"No, I'm fine," she protested.

"I want to."

"Really, Gregory, I'd rather—"

"Am I supposed to walk?" Suzanne interrupted.

Gregory turned to her. "I'll take you first, Suzanne, and then—"

"But I'm all right," Ivy insisted.

"She's all right," Suzanne echoed. "She is, I can tell. And we had plans."

"Suzanne, after what just happened, you can't expect me to leave Ivy alone. If Maggie's at home, then we can—"

"Could I give you a ride home, Ivy?" Will cut in.

"Yes. Thanks," she replied.

Gregory looked irritated.

Suzanne smiled. "Well, then, big brother," she said, putting her arm around Gregory, "it's all worked out. You have nothing to worry about."

"You'll stay with her?" Gregory asked Will. "You'll take care of her until Maggie gets home?"

"Sure." Will glanced up at the diving board. "Either I will or Tristan will," he added.

Ivy cocked her head at him. Suzanne giggled, then covered her mouth with her hand. Gregory didn't crack a smile.

4

"Oh, hi!" Beth said a few minutes later, looking up to see Ivy and Will. She was sitting against Ivy's locker, pencil in hand, looking as if she had been busily writing a story. But when Ivy glanced down at Beth's notebook, she knew better.

"If you write that way, you're going to have the end of the story at the beginning," Ivy said, leaning down and turning the notebook around.

Will laughed lightly, and Beth blushed.

"I guess I'm not much of an actress," she said, standing up. "You okay?"

Ivy shrugged. "I don't know how to answer that question anymore—and when I do, no one believes me anyway."

"She's okay," Will said, laying his hand on Beth's shoulder, reassuring her. Oddly enough, his confident tone reassured Ivy too.

She gathered her books, and the three of them headed out to the parking lot. Beth walked between Ivy and Will, keeping the conversation going. But a few minutes later, when Beth drove off, Ivy and Will fell into an uncomfortable silence. Ivy climbed into his silver Honda and kept her eyes straight ahead. As they headed toward her house the only thing he asked was whether she wanted the windows up.

Since the party Will had been avoiding Ivy at school. She figured he was probably embarrassed about their strange conversation on the dance floor. And she was grateful to him for swallowing his pride enough to get her out of a jam with Gregory and Suzanne.

"Thanks again," Ivy said.

"No problem," Will replied, adjusting the sun visor.

Ivy wondered why he didn't ask for an explanation of what she had been doing up on the diving board. Maybe he just assumed It was what crazy people did. As he drove he kept his eyes on the traffic. When they stopped at an intersection, Will seemed unusually attentive to the people crossing in front of the car. Then he stole a sidelong glance at her.

"That was a joke, wasn't it?" Ivy blurted out. "When you told Gregory that you'd take care of me—or Tristan would—you were just making a joke."

The light changed, and Will drove a block before answering. "Gregory didn't laugh," he observed.

"Were you making a joke?" Ivy persisted, twisting around in her seat.

"What do you think?"

47

"What does it matter what I think?" Ivy exploded. "I'm the crazy girl who tried to kill herself."

Will turned the wheel suddenly and pulled over to the side of the road. "I don't believe that," he said quietly.

"Well, everyone else does."

He kept the motor running and rested his arms on the wheel. Ivy studied the flecks of paint on his hands. "Some people may have bought the rumors," he said, "but I'm surprised you would."

She didn't say anything.

"It seems to me"—his voice was calm and reasonable—"that *really* crazy people don't think they're crazy. Why would you?"

"Well, there is that little story about my showing up at a train station," Ivy replied, unable to stop the sarcasm in her voice, "just before the late-night express rushed through."

He turned to her, his dark eyes challenging her. "Do you remember driving yourself there? Do you remember planning to jump in front of the train?"

Ivy shook her head. "No. None of that. I only remember the light afterward. The shimmering."

"Which is what you saw up on the diving board."

She nodded.

"I wonder why you see him and I hear him," Will said.

"You hear him?" Ivy reached over and switched off the motor. "You hear him?"

"So does Beth."

Ivy's mouth dropped open.

"She writes stories with messages that aren't hers. I draw angels I don't mean to draw." He drew an invisible image on the windshield. "We both thought we were losing it."

Ivy remembered the day at the electronics store, when Beth had typed on a computer: "Be careful, Ivy. It's dangerous, Ivy. Don't stay alone. Love you. Tristan." Ivy had run from the shop, furious at Beth for playing that trick. But she should have listened. Days later, she had been attacked at the house.

"He's warning you," Will continued. "Beth thinks it's something bigger than any of us can handle on our own, and she's scared to death."

Ivy felt the skin prickle on the back of her neck. Since the evening before, all she had thought about was reaching out toward the light that she believed was Tristan. She'd avoided the frightening question about why an angelic Tristan might be trying to reach her.

"You have to remember what happened," Will went on. "That's what Tristan was trying to tell you the night of the party, when we were dancing."

"He was with you then?" In her mind Ivy began to run through all the strange events of the past summer. "So the angels you drew, and that picture of an angel who looked like Tristan—"

"I was as amazed as you," Will said. "I tried to tell you, I'd never do something like that to hurt you. But I didn't know how to explain what happened. He got inside me. It was as if all I could do was draw those angels. My hands hardly felt like my own."

She reached over and laid her hand on his.

"I think he meant to comfort you," Will added.

Ivy nodded and blinked back tears. "I'm sorry I didn't understand then. I'm sorry I got so angry at you." She took a deep breath. "I have to remember. I have to go back to that night. Will, would you take me to the train station?"

He started the car immediately. When they arrived, several people had just gotten off a commuter train from New York City. Will parked the car as the station emptied out. Then he walked with Ivy as far as the steps to the southbound platform. "I'm not going to say anything more," he said. "It's probably best if you poke around on your own and see what comes to you. But I'll be right here if you need me."

Ivy nodded, then climbed the steps. From the police report she knew which pillar Philip had found her leaning against—propped up against, she corrected herself: the one labeled D. But she had forgotten how close the metal pillars were to the edge of the platform and how close the platform was to the track. When she saw it, her stomach lurched.

She knew she should stand with her back against the pillar and try to remember how it had been that night, but she couldn't do it, not yet. She hurried along the platform to the steps that led to the bridge over the tracks. Then she crossed the bridge to the other side. From the northbound platform, Ivy looked back at Will, who was sitting on a bench, waiting patiently for her.

She began to pace around. Who could have been there that night? If Philip's story was true, someone had dressed up like Tristan. Almost anyone could have gotten their hands on a school jacket and baseball cap. And wearing them half in the shadows, anyone could have looked like Tristan—including Gregory.

She backed away quickly from that thought. She was getting paranoid, suspecting Gregory. But maybe it wasn't so paranoid to imagine Eric doing it. She remembered the night he had drawn Will onto the railroad bridge just before a train came. Eric got his kicks out of dangerous games. And Eric definitely had access to drugs.

A long, shrill sound broke in on Ivy's thoughts, a whistle from a train headed south, echoing against the steep wall of the ridge. She looked back over her shoulder at the rocky hillside. It seemed impossible that Philip could have made it down safely, but maybe if angels were real, if Tristan was there . . .

The whistle sounded again. Ivy started to run. She took the steps two at a time, then raced across the bridge and down the other side. She could hear the rumbling of the train before she saw its headlight, a pale, blind eye in the daytime. It was one of the big Amtraks that would rush straight through.

She ran to the pillar and stood with her back to it, close to the edge, transfixed by the train's white eye. Her heart beat faster and faster as the train sped toward her. She remembered Philip's old story about a train climbing up the hill—a train that was seeking her. It thundered toward her now, its lines sparking, the platform beneath her vibrating. She felt as if her shaking body would fly apart.

Then the train blew by her in one long blur.

Ivy didn't know how long he had been standing there, close behind her, letting her knot her fingers in his. She turned her head sideways, looking at Will over her shoulder.

"I'm glad you didn't jump," he said with a half smile. "We both would have gone."

Ivy loosened her fingers and turned to face him.

"Do you remember now?" Will asked.

She shook her head wearily. "No."

Will lifted his arm as if he might touch her cheek. She looked up at him, and he pulled his hand back quickly, digging it into his pocket. "Let's get out of here," he said.

Ivy followed him to the car, continually glancing back at the tracks.

What if Gregory and Eric had worked together? she thought. But she still couldn't believe that anybody, least of all Gregory, would want to hurt her. He cared about her—she'd thought he cared deeply.

They drove out of the parking lot silently, Will apparently as deep in thought as she. Then Ivy sat up quickly and pointed. About fifty yards past the exit, a red Harley was parked on the side of the road. "It looks like Eric's," she said.

"It is."

A long drainage ditch with high grass and shrubs

bordered the road. Eric was searching the ditch and was so intent on his task that he didn't notice the car pulling over on the road's shoulder.

When Will opened the door, Eric's head bobbed up. "Lose something?" Will asked, stepping out. "Need some help looking?"

Eric screened his eyes against the slant of the sun. "No, thanks, Will," he called back. "I'm just trying to find an old bungee cord I use to tie things down." Then he noticed Ivy in the car. He seemed startled, glancing from her to Will and back again. He waved them on. "I'm giving up in a minute," he said.

Will nodded and got back into the car.

"He was looking awfully hard for an old bungee cord," Ivy remarked as they drove away.

"Ivy," Will said, "is there any reason why somebody would want to scare you or hurt you?"

"What do you mean?"

"Is anyone holding a grudge against you?"

"No," she replied slowly. There isn't anyone now, she thought. The past winter had been a different story: Gregory hadn't been at all happy about his father's marriage to Maggie. But his resentment and anger had disappeared months ago, she reminded herself quickly. Gregory had been wonderful to her since Tristan died, comforting her, even rescuing her the day of the break-in. It was Gregory who had gotten there first, scaring off the intruder, pulling the bag off her head just when Will arrived.

Or had he? Maybe he had been there all along.

His excuse for returning home that day had been an odd one. Suddenly Ivy felt cold all over. What if Gregory himself had attacked her, then changed plans when Will showed up?

The thought ran through her like an icy river, and her scalp and the skin on the back of her neck crawled. Ivy twisted her hands. Without realizing it, she bent a pen she had picked up from the car seat, cracking its plastic shell.

"Here," Will said, taking the pen away from her and offering her his hand. "I'll need my fingers back when we get to your house," he said, smiling, "but for now you won't get ink all over you."

Ivy gripped his hand. She held on tightly to Will and turned her head to watch bright patches of green flickering past them, the end of summer spliced with sharp shadows of fall.

"I've always been there for you. I love you." The words floated back to her. "Will, when we were dancing and Tristan was inside you, and you said—" She hesitated.

"And I said . . . ?"

"'I've always been there for you. I love you.'" She saw Will swallow hard. "It was Tristan speaking, right?" Ivy said. "It was just Tristan saying that, and I misunderstood. Right?"

Will watched a wishbone of geese flying across the sky. "Right," he said at last.

Neither of them spoke the rest of the way home.

5

Ivy stood next to Philip in his room, surveying a bookcase full of treasures: the angel statues she had given him after Tristan died, a stand-up paper doll of Don Mattingly, fossils from Andrew, and a rusty railroad spike.

Philip and Maggie had arrived home that afternoon just as Will was dropping off Ivy. After Ivy and Philip shared a snack, she'd scooped up his schoolbooks while he carefully carried his newest treasure, a moldy bird's nest, up to his room. Ivy watched him install the nest in a place of honor, then she ran her hand down the line of angel statues. She touched one that wasn't her own, an angel in a baseball uniform with wings.

"That's the statue Tristan's friend brought me," Philip told her. "I mean the girl angel. I've seen her a couple of times."

"You've seen another angel? Are you sure?" Ivy asked, surprised.

Philip nodded. "She came to our big party."

"How can you tell her apart from Tristan?" Ivy wondered.

Philip thought for a moment. "Her colors are more purplish."

"How do you know she's a girl?"

"She's shaped like one," he said.

"Oh."

"Like a girl your age," he added. From beneath a stack of comic books, Philip dug out a photograph with a strange pale blur in it. Ivy recognized the picture: it was the first photo that Will had taken of them at the arts festival.

Philip studied it and frowned. "I guess you can't see as much here," he said.

See as much what? Ivy wondered silently.

"Do you really want just your water angel back?" Philip asked.

Ivy knew he wanted to keep all the statues. "Just her," she assured him, then carried the porcelain angel into her own room. This was the statue Ivy loved most. Its swirling blue-green robe had prompted her to name it after the angel she had seen when she was four, the angel who had saved her from drowning. Ivy set the statue next to Tristan's picture, running her hand over the angel's smooth glazed surface. Then she touched Tristan's photo.

"Two angels—my two angels," she said,

then headed up to her third-floor music room.

Ella followed her and leaped up into the dormer window across from Ivy's piano. Ivy sat down and began to work through her scales, sending out ripples of music. As her hands moved up and down the keyboard, she thought about Tristan, the way he'd looked when he swam, light scattered in the water drops around him, the way his light could shine around her now.

The late sunlight of September was a pure gold like his shimmer, and the sunset would have the same rim of colors. Ivy glanced toward the window and stopped playing abruptly. Ella was sitting up, her ears alert, her eyes big and shiny. Ivy turned quickly to look behind her. "Tristan," she said softly.

The glow surrounded her.

"Tristan," she whispered again. "Talk to me. Why can't I hear you? The others hear you—Will and Beth. Can't you speak to me?"

But the only sound was the light thump of Ella leaping down from her perch and trotting over to her. Ivy wondered if the cat could see Tristan.

"Yes, she saw me the first time I came."

Ivy was stunned by his voice. "It's you. You really are—"

"Amazing, isn't it?"

Within herself, Ivy could hear not only his voice but also the laughter in it. He sounded just as he always had when something amused him. Then the laughing ceased.

"Ivy, I love you. I'll never stop loving you."

Ivy laid her face down in her hands. Her palms and fingers were bathed in pale golden light. "I love you, Tristan, and I've missed you. You don't know how much I've missed you."

"You don't know how often I've been with you, watching you sleep, listening to you play. It was like last winter all over again, waiting and wanting, hoping you'd notice me."

The yearning in his voice made Ivy quiver inside, the way his kisses once had.

"If I'd had the right angelic powers, I would have thrown some broccoli and carrots at you," he added, laughing.

Ivy laughed, too, remembering the tray of vegetables he'd overturned at her mother's wedding.

"It was the carrots in your ears and the shrimp tails up your nose that made you irresistible to both Philip and me," she said, smiling. "Oh, Tristan, I wish we'd had this summer together. I wish we could have floated side by side in the center of the lake, letting the sun sparkle at our fingers and toes."

"All I want is to be close to you," Tristan told her.

Ivy lifted her head. "I wish I could feel your arms around me."

"You couldn't get any closer to my heart than you are now."

Ivy held out her arms, then folded them around herself like closed wings. "I've wished a thousand times that I could tell you I love you. But I never believed, I just never believed I'd be given a chance—"

"You have to believe, Ivy!" She heard the fear in his voice ringing inside her. "Don't stop believing, or you'll stop seeing me. You need me now, in ways that you don't know," he warned.

"Because of Gregory," she said, dropping her hands in her lap. "I do know. I just don't understand why he would want to"—she backed away from the most terrifying thought—"to hurt me."

"To *kill* you," said Tristan. "Everything that Philip described about that night happened, only 'the bad angel' was Gregory. And it wasn't the first time, Ivy. When you were alone that weekend—"

"But it doesn't make sense," she cried, "not after all he's done for me." She jumped up from the piano bench and began to pace around the room. "After the accident, he was the only one who understood why I didn't want to talk about it."

"He didn't want you to think too much," Tristan replied. "He didn't want you to remember that night and start asking questions—such as whether our accident was an accident."

Ivy paused by the window. Three stories below her, Philip was kicking a soccer ball. Andrew, coming up the driveway, had stopped the car to watch. Her mother was walking across the grass toward him.

"It wasn't an accident," she said at last. She remembered her nightmare: she was in Tristan's car, and she couldn't stop—just like the night they'd hit the deer and couldn't stop. "Someone fooled with the brakes."

"It looks that way."

Ivy felt sick to her stomach at just the thought of Gregory touching her, kissing her, holding her close, close enough to kill her when the chance arose. She didn't want to believe it. "Why?" she cried.

"I think it goes back to the night of Caroline's murder."

Ivy walked back to the piano and sat down slowly, trying to sort things out. "You mean he blames me for his mother's—his mother's *murder?* It was suicide, Tristan." But as she said it she could feel a numbness in her chest and throat, a growing fear that threatened to shut down every reasonable thought.

"You were at the house next door on the night she died," Tristan told her. "I think you saw someone in the window, someone who knows what happened or was responsible for it. Try to remember."

Ivy struggled to separate her memory of the night from the nightmares that had followed. "All I could see was a shadow of a person. With all the reflections on the glass, I never saw who it was."

"But he saw you."

Bit by bit, the dream was unraveling. Ivy began to shake.

"I know," Tristan said gently. "I know."

Ivy longed to feel the touch that she had once felt when he spoke to her that way.

"I'm afraid, too," Tristan said. "I don't have the powers to protect you by myself. But believe me, Ivy, together we're stronger than he is."

"Oh, Tristan, I've missed you."

"I've missed you," he replied, "missed holding you, kissing you, making you mad . . ."

She laughed.

"Ivy, play for me."

"Don't—don't ask me that now. I just want to keep hearing your voice," she pleaded. "I thought I had lost you forever, but now you're here—"

"Shhh, Ivy. Play. I heard a noise. Someone's in your bedroom."

Ivy glanced at Ella, who stood at the top of the steps now, peering down into the darkness. The cat crept quietly down the stairs, her tail bristling. It's Gregory, Ivy thought.

She nervously opened a book and began to play. Ivy played loudly, trying to blot out the memories of Gregory's embraces, his urgent kisses, the night they had been alone in the store and the night they had been alone in the darkened house.

Trying to kill her? Killing his mother? It didn't make sense. She could almost understand how Eric could do it, half crazed with drugs. She remembered the message she'd overheard on Gregory's phone; Eric was always in need of drug money. Maybe he had tried to get some from Caroline, and things went wrong. But what motive would Gregory have had for such a terrible thing?

"That's what I've been trying to figure out."

Ivy stopped playing for a moment. "You can hear me?" she asked silently.

"You don't cloak your thoughts as well as Will."

So he had heard everything she had just thought, including the part about the urgent kisses. Ivy began playing again, banging on the piano.

Tristan sounded as if he were shouting in her head. "I guess I shouldn't have been listening in, huh?"

She smiled and softened the music.

"Ivy, we need to be honest with each other. If we can't trust each other, who else can we depend on?"

"I love you. That's honest," Ivy said, speaking all her words silently now, so only Tristan could hear. She finished the song and was about to start another.

"He's gone," Tristan told her.

Ivy breathed a sigh of relief.

"Listen to me, Ivy. You've got to get out of here."

"Get out? What do you mean?" she asked.

"You have to get as far away from Gregory as you can."

"That's impossible," Ivy said. "I can't just get up and leave. I have nowhere to go."

"You'll find somewhere. And I'll ask Lacey—she's an angel—to stay near you. Until I can figure out what's going on and come up with some evidence to take to the police, you have to get away from here."

"No," Ivy said, pushing back the piano bench.

"Yes," he insisted. Then he told her about what he had learned from time-traveling through the minds of Gregory and Eric. He recounted the angry scene between Gregory and his mother, how Caroline had taunted him with a piece of paper, and how he'd shoved the floor lamp at her, cutting her face. Then

Tristan told Ivy about the memory he had experienced in Eric's mind, the intense scene between him and Caroline, which had taken place on a stormy evening.

"You're right about Eric," Tristan concluded. "He needs drug money and he's involved. But I still don't know exactly what he's done for Gregory."

"Eric was searching the gully by the station today," Ivy said.

"He was? Then he took Gregory's threat seriously," Tristan replied, and recounted the argument he had overheard at the party. "I'll watch both of them. In the meantime, you need to get away."

"No," Ivy repeated.

"Yes, as soon as possible."

"No!" This time the voice leaped out of her.

Tristan fell silent.

"I'm not leaving," she said, speaking within her mind again. Ivy walked to the window and gazed out at the old and windblown trees that topped the ridge, trees that had become familiar to her in the last six months. She had watched them change from a spring mist of red buds to dense, green leaves to delicate shapes traced with the gold of the evening sun—the color of autumn. This was her home, this was where the people she loved were. She wasn't going to be chased away. She wasn't going to leave Philip and Suzanne alone with Gregory.

"Suzanne doesn't know anything," Tristan said. "After you left with Will today, I followed her and Gregory. She's innocent—confused about you and totally hooked on him."

"Totally hooked on Gregory, and you want me to leave her?"

"She doesn't know enough to get herself in trouble," Tristan argued.

"If I run away," Ivy persisted, "how do we know what he'll do? How do we know he won't go after Philip? Philip may not understand what he saw, but he saw things that night, things that won't make Gregory very happy."

Tristan was silent.

"I can't see you," Ivy said, "but I can guess what kind of a face you're making."

Then she heard him laugh, and she started laughing with him.

"Oh, Tristan, I know you love me and are afraid for me, but I can't leave them. Philip and Suzanne don't know that Gregory's dangerous. They won't be on guard around him."

He didn't reply.

"Are you there?" she asked after a long silence.

"Just thinking," he said.

"Then you're cloaking," she said. "You're keeping your thoughts from me."

Suddenly Ivy was rocked with feelings of love and tenderness. Then intense fear rushed through her, and anger, and wordless despair. She was swimming in a churning sea of emotions, and for a moment she couldn't breathe.

"Maybe I should have lifted just one corner of the cloak," Tristan remarked. "I have to leave you now, Ivy."

"No. Wait. When will I see you again?" she asked. "How will I find you?"

"Well, you don't have to stand on the end of a diving board."

Ivy smiled.

"The end of a tree limb will do," he said. "Or the roof of any building three stories or higher."

"What?"

"Just kidding," he said, laughing. "Just call—anytime, anywhere, silently—and I'll hear you. If I don't come, it's because I'm in the middle of something that I can't stop, or I'm in the darkness. I can't control the darkness." He sighed. "I can feel it coming on—I can feel it right now—and I can fight it off for a while. But in the end I fall unconscious. It's how I rest. I guess one day the darkness will be final."

"No!"

"Yes, love," he said softly.

A moment later he was gone.

The emptiness he left inside her was almost unbearable. Without his light, the room fell into blue shadow and Ivy felt lost in the twilight between two worlds. She fought against the doubts that began to creep in. She hadn't imagined this—Tristan was there, and Tristan would come back again.

She worked through some Bach pieces, playing them mechanically one after another, and had just closed her music books when her mother called up to her. Maggie's voice sounded funny, and when Ivy reached the bottom of the steps she saw why.

Maggie was standing in front of Ivy's bureau; the water angel lay shattered at her feet.

"Honey, I'm sorry," her mother said.

Ivy walked over to the bureau and got down on her knees. There were a few large pieces, but the rest of the statue had splintered into small fragments. It could never be repaired.

"Philip must have left it here," Maggie said. "He must have put it too close to the edge. Please don't let this upset you, honey."

"I brought it in here myself, Mom. And it's nothing to get upset about. Accidents happen," she said, marveling at her own calmness. "Please don't blame yourself."

"But I didn't do it," Maggie replied quickly. "I walked in to call you for dinner and saw it lying here."

Hearing their voices, Philip stuck his head in the door. "Oh, no!" he wailed. "She broke!"

Gregory came into the room behind him. He looked at the statue, then shook his head, glancing over at the bed. "Ella," he said softly.

But Ivy knew who had done it. It was the same person who had shredded Andrew's expensive chair months ago—and it wasn't Ella. She wanted to charge across the room. She wanted to back Gregory against the wall. She wanted to make him admit it in front of the others. But she knew she had to play along. And she would—till she got him to confess that he had broken more things than porcelain angels.

6

"'Tis the Season, Ivy speaking. How can I help you?"

"Did you find out?"

"Suzanne! I told you not to call me at work unless it's an emergency. You know we have a Friday night special," Ivy said, and glanced toward the door, where two customers had just come in. The little shop, filled to the brim with costumes and a hodgepodge of out-of-season items—Easter baskets, squeaking turkeys, and plastic menorahs—always attracted shoppers. Betty, one of the two old sisters who owned the shop, was home sick, and Lillian and Ivy had their hands full.

"This *is* an emergency," Suzanne insisted. "Did you find out who Gregory's going out with tonight?"

"I don't even know if he's got a date. I came here right after school, so I have nothing new to tell you since we talked at three o'clock."

Ivy wished Suzanne hadn't called. In the twenty-four

hours since Tristan had visited her, she had been on the alert no matter where she was. At home, Gregory's bedroom door was right down the hall from hers. At school, she saw him all the time. It had been a relief to come to work: she felt safe among the crowd of customers and was glad not to think about Gregory, even if it was for only six hours.

"Well, you sure are a lousy detective," Suzanne said, her laughter breaking in on Ivy's thoughts. "As soon as you get home tonight, start snooping. Philip may know something. I want to know who and where, for how long, and what she wore."

"Listen, Suzanne," Ivy said, "I don't want to be the one carrying stories back and forth between you and Gregory. Even if I knew that Gregory was with somebody else tonight, I wouldn't feel right telling you that, any more than I'd feel right telling him that you're with Jeff."

"But you've got to tell him, Ivy!" Suzanne exclaimed. "That's the whole point! How is he going to get jealous if he doesn't know?"

Ivy silently shook her head and watched three young boys jabbing pencils into the store's seven-foot model of King Kong. "I've got customers, Suzanne. I've got to go."

"Did you hear what I said? I want to make Gregory incredibly jealous."

"We'll talk later, okay?"

"Outrageously jealous," Suzanne said. "So jealous, he can't see straight."

"We'll talk later," Ivy said, hanging up.

Each time she finished with a customer that evening, Ivy's thoughts drifted back to Suzanne. If Suzanne made Gregory outrageously jealous, would he hurt her? She wished Suzanne and Gregory would lose interest in each other, but this on-again off-again stuff was just the kind of thing to keep the fire burning.

If I tell Suzanne he's going out with a hundred different girls, Ivy thought, she'll want him all the more. If I criticize him, she'll just defend him and get mad at me.

At closing time Lillian sat down wearily on the stool behind the cash register. She shut her eyes for a moment.

"You okay?" Ivy asked. "You look pretty tired."

The old woman patted Ivy's hand. Her mother's diamond ring, a pink healing crystal, and a Star Trek communicator glittered on her gnarled fingers. "I'm fine, dear, fine. I'm nothing but old," she said.

"Why don't you rest a few minutes? I can do the receipts," Ivy told her, taking the pile away from the owner. After they closed up, Ivy planned to walk Lillian to her car. Once the customers left and the lights were dimmed, the cavernous mall would be filled with shadows and small rustlings. That night Ivy would be as glad as Lillian to have some company.

"I'm nothing but ancient," Lillian said with a sigh. "Ivy, would you do me a favor? Would you close up tonight?"

"Close up?" Ivy was caught by surprise. Stay by myself? she thought. "Sure."

Lillian got up from the stool and put on her sweater. "Come in late tomorrow, lovey," she said as she walked toward the door. "Betty should be on her feet again, and we'll be all right. You're a dear."

"It's no trouble," Ivy said softly as she watched Lillian disappear into the mall. She wondered where Tristan was, and if she should call him.

Don't be such a coward, Ivy chided herself, and turned to open the wall box where the light switches were. She hit the switches, dimming all the store's lights, then changed her mind and turned half of them back on again. Ivy glanced toward the dressing rooms at the back of the store. She fought the urge to double-check and make sure everyone was out. Don't be so paranoid, she told herself. But it wasn't hard to imagine someone lurking in a fitting room, and it wasn't hard to picture someone waiting for her in the shadows of the mall.

"I want everything in your cash box."

Ivy jumped at the sound of Eric's voice. His finger poked her in the back. Someone else laughed—Gregory.

She spun around to face both of them.

"Oh, sorry," Gregory said when he saw the look on her face. "We didn't mean to really scare you."

"I meant to," Eric said with a high-pitched laugh.

"We thought you'd be finishing up soon, so we stopped by," Gregory said, touching her on the elbow, his voice soft and easy.

"To get your cash before you put it in the safe," Eric interjected. "About how much do you have?"

"Ignore him," Gregory told Ivy.

70

"She does. She always has," Eric remarked, and started rifling through the shop's bins.

"We're just hanging out tonight," Gregory said. "Want to hang out with us?"

Ivy forced a smile and flipped through the store receipts. "Thanks, but I've got a lot to do."

"We'll wait."

She smiled again and shook her head.

"Come on, Ivy," Gregory urged. "You've hardly been out in the last three weeks. It'll be good for you."

"Will it?" Ivy looked up, gazing directly into Gregory's eyes. "You're always looking out for me."

"And I'll continue to," he replied, smiling at her. There wasn't a hint of what he was thinking behind his gray eyes and too-handsome face.

"Teeth!" Eric exclaimed. "Look at these blood-sucking teeth. This is cool." He ripped open a plastic package and stuck the vampire teeth in his mouth, grinning at Gregory. His skinny arms dangled by his sides, and his fingers danced with nervousness. Ivy thought about the way Gregory had applauded Eric the night his friend conned them at the railroad bridges. She wondered how far Eric would go to amuse Gregory and win his approval.

"It's an improvement, Eric," Gregory said, "and some girls get turned on by vampires." He gave Ivy a sly smile. "Don't they?"

The last time Gregory had come late to the shop, he had dressed up as Dracula. Ivy remembered his insistent kisses and how she had given in to them.

Now her skin grew warm, and she could feel herself flushing with anger. Her fingers curled into fists, which she quickly put behind her.

I can play this game as well as he can, she thought, and tilted back her head. "Some girls do."

Gregory stared at her neck, his eyes glimmering, then focused on her mouth, as if he wanted to kiss her again.

"Ivy, what in the world are you doing?"

The question stunned her. It was Tristan's voice. She hadn't been aware of him slipping inside her mind, yet clearly neither Eric nor Gregory had heard him speak. Ivy knew her face was red, and she quickly dropped her chin.

Gregory laughed. "You're blushing."

Ivy turned and walked away from him. But she couldn't get away from Tristan.

"You think he wants to kiss you?" Tristan asked scornfully. "Strangle you, maybe! Ivy, don't be stupid. These are tricks."

Silently she told Tristan, "I know what I'm doing."

Gregory followed her over to the counter and slid his hand around her waist.

"Gregory, please," she said.

"Please what?" he asked, his mouth close to her ear.

"Eric is here," she reminded him, and glanced over her shoulder. But Eric was on the other side of a rack, lost in a world of costumes.

"My mistake," Gregory said softly, "bringing Eric along."

"Get rid of Gregory," Tristan cut in. "Get rid of both of them and lock the door."

Ivy slid away from Gregory.

"Call security," Tristan continued. "Ask them to walk you to your car."

"Besides," Ivy said to Gregory, "there's Suzanne. You know Suzanne and I have been friends forever."

"Ivy!" Tristan exclaimed. "Don't you know anything about guys? You're setting yourself up. Now he's going to use one of those old excuses."

Ivy silently retorted, "I know what I'm doing."

"Suzanne is too easy," Gregory said, moving closer to Ivy. "Too jealous and too easy. I'm bored."

"I guess it's a lot more interesting," Tristan remarked, "to get it on with the girlfriend of the guy you murdered."

Ivy jerked her head as if she had been slapped.

"What's wrong?" Gregory asked her.

"Ivy, I'm sorry," Tristan said quickly, "but you're not listening to me. You don't seem to understand—"

"I understand, Tristan," Ivy thought angrily. "Leave me alone before I mess up."

"What are you thinking?" Gregory asked. "You're mad, I can tell." He smoothed her brow, then traced her cheek, his fingers lightly touching her neck. "You used to like it when I touched you," he said.

Ivy could feel Tristan's anger surging up inside her. She felt as if she was losing control. She closed her eyes, focused her attention, and pressed him out, out as far as she could from her mind.

When she opened her eyes Gregory was staring at her. "Out?" he said. "Were you talking to me?"

"Talking to you?" Ivy echoed. Terrific. She had spoken aloud. "No," she told Gregory, "I don't remember saying anything to you."

He frowned at her.

"But you know me," she said cheerfully, "I'm just a little crazy."

He continued to stare at her. "Maybe," he said.

Ivy smiled and moved past him. For the next fifteen minutes she paid attention to Eric, helping him find parts of costumes, while keeping one eye on the shop door, waiting for security to pass by. When the guard did and pointed to his watch, signaling that it was well past nine-thirty, she called out to him. Since the mall was officially closed, she asked him if he'd show Eric and Gregory a door where they could exit.

Then she locked the shop door behind them and leaned back against it, limp with relief. "I'm sorry, Tristan," she said, but she was pretty sure he didn't hear her.

Tristan watched Ivy, her head bent over the store receipts, her curly hair a web of gold under the one light that now shone over the desk at the cash register. The rest of the shop was dimly lit, its corners receding into darkness.

He wanted to touch her hair, to materialize his fingers and feel the softness of her skin. He wanted to talk to her, just talk to her. But he remained hidden, still angry, hurt by the way she had thrust him out of her mind.

Ivy raised her head suddenly and glanced around as if she sensed his presence. "Tristan?"

If he stayed outside of her, she wouldn't hear him. But what did he have to say to her? That he loved her. That she had hurt him. That he was terrified for her.

She saw him now. "Tristan." The way she said his name could still make him tremble. "I didn't think you'd come back. After putting you out like that, I didn't think you'd come to me."

Tristan stayed where he was.

"And you're not coming to me, are you?" she asked.

He heard the tremor in her voice and couldn't decide what to do. Leave her? Let her wonder for a while. He didn't want to fight, and he had work to do that night.

If only you knew how much I love you, he thought.

"Tristan," she said silently.

He was in her mind now and knew the thought they had shared: If only you knew how much I love you.

Ivy was crying.

"Don't. Please don't," he said.

"Try to understand," she begged him silently. "I gave my heart to you, but it's still mine. You can't just come in and take over. I have my own thoughts, Tristan, and my own way of doing things."

"You've always had your own thoughts and your own way of doing things," he said. Then he laughed in spite of himself. "I remember how you were leading your guide around your very first day in our school—that's when I fell in love with you," he told her. "But you've got to understand, too. I'm afraid for you. What were you doing, Ivy, playing like that with Gregory?"

Ivy slid off the desk stool and walked toward a dark corner of the shop. Eric had left a pile of costumes on the floor. Tristan could feel their silky softness through Ivy's hands as she picked them up. "I'm playing Gregory's game," she said. "I'm playing the role he's given me—keeping him wondering and keeping him close."

"It's too dangerous, Ivy."

"No," she replied firmly. "Living in the same house with him and trying to avoid him—that would be dangerous. I can't hide from him, so the trick is never, ever to take my eyes off him." She picked up a glittering black mask and held it in front of her face.

"I have to know what he's doing and what he's saying," she continued. "I have to wait for him to slip up. As long as I'm here—and I told you, Tristan, I'm staying here—it's the only way."

"There's another way to keep track of him," Tristan said, "and to keep a person between you at the same time. Will is his friend. You could date Will."

There was a long silence, and Tristan could feel Ivy cloaking her thoughts from him. "No, that's not a good idea," she said at last.

"Why not?" His voice came out too sharply. He could feel her searching carefully for the right words.

"I don't want to get Will involved."

"But he already is," Tristan argued. "He knows about me. He took you to the train station to help you remember what happened."

"That's as far as it goes," Ivy said. "I don't want you to tell him anything else." She started sorting through the costumes, shaking them out, then folding them.

"You're protecting him," Tristan said.

"That's right."

"Why?" he asked.

"Why put someone else in danger?" she replied.

"Will would put himself in any kind of danger for you. He's in love with you." As soon as Tristan said it he wished that he hadn't.

But certainly Ivy had already figured that out. Maybe not, he thought suddenly. He felt her struggling. He was caught in a swirl of emotions that he couldn't understand. He knew she was confused.

"I don't think so," Ivy said. "Will's a friend, that's all."

Tristan didn't say anything.

"But if it is true, Tristan, then it's not fair to use him like that. It'd be leading him on."

Would it really? Tristan wondered. Maybe Ivy was afraid to admit her attraction to Will.

"What are you thinking? What are you cloaking?" Ivy asked.

"I'm wondering if you're being honest with yourself."

Ivy walked briskly across the shop, as if she could walk away from him, hanging up the costumes, tossing misplaced objects into their bins. "I don't know why you think the way you do. It's almost as if you're jealous," she said.

"I am," he replied.

"You're what?" Her voice sounded frustrated.

"Jealous." There was no point in trying to hide it, Tristan thought.

"Who said that?" Ivy demanded.

"Who said what?" Tristan asked.

"Who said what?" a female voice echoed, the same voice that had sounded frustrated a moment ago.

"Lacey!" Tristan exclaimed. He hadn't seen her come in.

"Yes, sweetie?" Lacey was projecting her voice so Ivy could hear it, too. Ivy glanced around the room.

"This is a private conversation," Tristan said.

"Well, her half was private," Lacey replied, still projecting her voice. "When your chick speaks inwardly, I can hear only your part. Talk about frustrating! This year's romantic smash, and I'm missing half the dialogue. Ask your chick to speak out loud, okay?"

"Your chick?" Ivy repeated aloud.

"That's better," said Lacey.

"Is she that purplish blob?" Ivy asked.

"*Ex-cuuuse* me?" Lacey said.

Tristan could feel a headache coming on. "Yes, that's her," he told Ivy.

"A blob?" Lacey spit out the word.

"That's how you look to Ivy," Tristan said. "You know that."

"How does she look to you?" Ivy asked Tristan. He hesitated.

"Yes, tell us both, how do I look to you?" Lacey asked.

Tristan tried to think of an objective description. "Like . . . five foot something . . . with brown eyes, I think . . . and a roundish nose, and sort of thick hair."

"Good job, Tristan," Lacey remarked. "You've just described a bear." To Ivy she said, "I'm Lacey Lovitt. Now I'm sure you can picture me."

Tristan could feel Ivy's mind searching, trying to remember who Lacey Lovitt was.

"The country-western star?"

A plastic turkey was hurled across the room. "And to think I *bothered* to come back to warn the chick."

"Why does she keep calling me the chick?"

"I guess it's movie star talk," Tristan said wearily.

"You were a movie star?" Ivy bent down to pick up the thrown turkey. "So you're pretty," Ivy said quietly.

"Ask Tristan," said Lacey.

"Is she?"

Tristan felt trapped. "I'm not a good judge of those things."

"Oh, I see," Ivy and Lacey said at the exact same time, both of them sounding irritated. Ivy paced one way, Lacey the other.

"How did you throw this, Lacey Lovitt?" Ivy asked, squeaking the turkey. "Can Tristan do it?"

79

Lacey snickered. "Not with any kind of aim," she said. "He's still learning to materialize his fingers, to make himself solid. He's got a lot to learn. Luckily he's got me as a teacher."

She moved closer to Ivy. Tristan could feel Ivy tingle when she felt Lacey's fingers resting lightly on her skin. Through Ivy's eyes he saw the long purple nails slowly appear on her arm.

"When Tristan slips back out of your mind," Lacey said, "he'll look and feel solid to me. But unless he materializes himself, like I just did, he'll be just a glow to you. It takes a lot of energy to materialize. He's getting stronger, but if he uses up too much energy, he'll fall into the darkness."

"He'll look and feel solid to you?" Ivy repeated.

"He can hold my hand, see my face," Lacey said. "He can—well, you know."

Tristan could feel Ivy prickling.

"But he hasn't," Lacey said bluntly. "He's *totally* hung up on you." She picked up a hat and spun it on a fingertip, lifting it above her head. To Ivy she looked like a lavender mist with a mysteriously spinning top hat. "You know, I could have a lot of fun haunting this place. I could get the old ladies some real publicity come Halloween."

"Don't even think about it," Tristan said.

"Forgive me if I forget that you said that," Lacey told him. "Anyway, I'm here to give you the skinny. Gregory's picked up some new drugs."

"When?" Tristan asked quickly.

"Tonight, just before he got here," Lacey replied, then said to Ivy, "Be careful what you eat. Be careful what you drink. Don't make it easy for him."

Ivy shivered.

"Thanks, Lacey," Tristan said. "I owe you—even though you did sneak in and listen to what was none of your business."

"Yeah, yeah."

"I'm the one who owes you," Ivy said.

"That's right," Lacey snapped, "and for more than just that! For the last two and a half months I've had to listen to enough heaving and sighing over you to fill three volumes of bad love poetry. And I've got to tell you—"

"Lacey's never been in love," Tristan interrupted, "so she doesn't understand—"

"Excuse me? Ex*cuse* me?" Lacey challenged him. "Do you know that for a fact?"

Tristan laughed.

"As I was saying . . ." Lacey moved closer to Ivy. "I just don't know what he sees in you."

Ivy was stung into a moment of silence. At last she replied, "Well, I know what he sees in you."

"Oh, *puh-lease*."

Ivy laughed and picked up a top hat, spinning it on her own fingertip. "Tristan's always been a sucker for girls with their own way of doing things."

7

Tristan lay quietly, listening to Eric's breathing and conserving his own energy, watching the sky outside the bedroom window beginning to lighten. The numbers on Eric's clock radio glowed: it was 4:46. As soon as Eric showed signs of stirring, Tristan planned to slip inside his mind.

He had checked on Eric Friday night, several hours after his visit to the mall, and Saturday night as well, after Eric came home from a drinking binge. Lacey had repeatedly warned Tristan about time-traveling in a mind confused by alcohol and bent by drugs. But it had been twenty-four hours since Eric's last beer, and Tristan was willing to take a chance to learn just what kind of dirty work Eric had done for Gregory.

He had lucked out when he arrived in Eric's room early Monday, discovering on one of his shelves an old book about trains. Materializing a finger, he had paged through the book, searching for a photo of a train that looked similar to those that ran through Stonehill's station. Now he watched Eric sleep, waiting for his chance to show him that picture and slip in on a shared thought. With a little more luck, he could ride the thought into a memory, the memory of the night Ivy had been drugged and taken to the station.

He waited patiently as the digital clock flashed the passing minutes. Eric's breathing was becoming shallow, and his legs grew restless—now was the time. Tristan nudged him awake. Eric saw the book on his pillow and pulled his head up sleepily, squinting at the picture.

Train, thought Tristan. Whistling. Slow down. Looks like an accident. Wasn't an accident. Gregory. Blew it. Chick, chick, chick, who wants to play chick, chick, chick?

Tristan ran through as many thoughts as he could that were related to the picture. He didn't know which thought was his ticket in, but he suddenly saw the photograph through Eric's half-closed eyes. Eric seemed just alert enough to take a suggestion. Tristan pictured as clearly as he could a baseball cap and school jacket, the ones that Gregory had worn that night, the ones that he had insisted Eric find.

Tristan felt Eric tense. For a moment he felt suspended in timeless darkness, then he pitched forward with him, his fist glancing off something hard. He was swiftly thrown backward, making him lose his balance, then was pushed forward once more.

Every muscle strained—Eric was fighting with someone. A sharp punch to his stomach made him lurch. Eric twisted his head around—Tristan twisted his—and saw his opponent: Gregory.

Tristan saw the road, too, as he spun with Eric one way, then the other, beneath Gregory's blows. He thought he was about thirty yards from the entrance to the train station. As he struggled with Gregory his feet kept slipping on small stones at the side of the road. Something sharp bit into his hand. Tristan realized suddenly that Eric was clinging to a set of keys.

"You dumb-ss." Tristan felt Eric's words slur in his mouth. "You can't drive my machine. You'll crash us and you'll kill us both. It'll be you, me, and Tristan forever, you, me, and Tristan forever, you, me, and Tristan—"

"Shut up. Give them to me," Gregory said, ripping the keys out of his hand, leaving his palm raw and bloody. "You can't even hold your head up."

Tristan suddenly felt as if he were going to be sick. Trapped inside the body of Eric, he leaned on the Harley, holding his stomach and breathing hard. Gregory fumbled with something on the back of the bike. He was trying to tie something to it—the jacket and cap.

"We've got to get out of here," Gregory said to him.

They struggled to climb onto the motorcycle. His leg felt unbearably heavy as he lifted it over the seat. Gregory shoved him toward the back of the machine, then climbed on the front.

"Hang on."

He did. When Gregory hit the accelerator, Tristan felt his head snap back. His upper jaw crunched down on his lower, and his eyes felt as small and hard as marbles rolling inside his head. In that brief moment he saw a blur behind him. He turned just as the clothes tumbled off the bike, but he didn't say anything.

They rode toward town, then up the long hill to Gregory's house. Gregory got off and rushed inside. Now the motorcycle was in Eric's hands—Tristan's hands, though he had no control. He raced down the hill again, driving crazily. Suddenly the road snaked out from under the wheels, and Eric was on another path.

Were they in another memory? Had they somehow linked up with another part of the past? The road, with its sharp twists and turns, seemed familiar to Tristan. The Harley skidded to a stop, and Tristan felt ill all over again: they were at the spot where he had died.

Eric parked and got off the motorcycle, surveying the road for several minutes. He stooped down to examine some sparkling blue stones—bits of shattered glass among the gravel in the road. Suddenly he reached over and picked up a bouquet of roses. They looked fresh, as if someone had just left them there, and were tied with a purple ribbon, the kind Ivy wore in her hair. Eric touched one rose that hadn't opened. A tremor ran through him.

One rose, unopened, stood in a vase on Caroline's table. Eric's mind had jumped again, and

Tristan knew he had been in this memory before. The picture window, the brewing storm outside, Eric's intense fear and growing frustration were all familiar to Tristan. Just as before, the memory ran like a piece of damaged film, frames spliced out, sound washed over by waves of emotion. Caroline was looking at him and laughing, laughing as if nothing in the world could be funnier. Suddenly he reached for her arms, grabbing her, shaking her, rocking her till her head flopped like a rag doll's.

"Listen to me," he said. "I mean it! It's not a joke! Nobody's laughing but you. It's not a joke!"

Then Eric groaned. It wasn't fear that rippled through him now. It wasn't frustration and anger burning out of his skin, but something deep and awful, despairing. He groaned again and opened his eyes. Tristan saw the book of trains in front of him.

The book looked blurry, and Eric passed his hand over his eyes. He was awake and crying. "Not again," he whispered. "Not again."

What did he mean? Tristan wondered. What didn't Eric want to happen again? What didn't he want to do again? Let Gregory kill? Let himself get out of control and do Gregory's killing for him? Maybe they had each done some of it and were tied together in a guilty knot.

Tristan struggled hard to remain conscious and stay with Eric through the rest of Monday morning. He had slipped out of Eric's mind the moment he was fully awake but accompanied him to school, guessing that the memories that haunted Eric would lead him toward some kind of confrontation with Gregory. He was caught off guard at lunchtime when Eric moved quickly through a crowded cafeteria toward the table where Ivy sat alone.

"I have to talk to you."

Ivy blinked up at him, surprised. His pale hair was matted. Over the summer, he had grown so thin that his white skin barely seemed to cover the bones of his face. The circles under his eyes looked like bruises.

When Ivy spoke, Tristan heard an unexpected gentleness in her voice. "Okay. Talk to me."

"Not here. Not with all these people."

Ivy glanced around the cafeteria. Tristan guessed that she was trying to decide how to handle this. He wanted to slip inside her and shout, "Don't do it! Don't go anywhere with him!" But he knew what would happen: She'd throw him out just as she had the last time.

"Can you tell me what this is about?" Ivy asked, her voice still soft.

"Not here," he said. His fingers played nervously on the tabletop.

"At my house, then," she suggested.

Eric shook his head. He kept glancing left and right.

Tristan saw with relief that Beth and Will were carrying their lunch trays toward Ivy's table. Eric saw them, too.

"There's an old car," he said quickly, "dumped about a half mile below the train bridges, just back from the river. I'll meet you there today, five o'clock. Come alone. I want to talk, but only if you're alone."

"But I—"

"Come alone. Don't tell anyone." He was already moving away from the table.

"Eric," she called after him. "Eric!"

He didn't turn back.

"What was that about?" Will asked as he set his tray on the table. He didn't seem aware of Tristan's presence. Neither did Beth or Ivy. Maybe none of them saw his light because of the sun flooding through the cafeteria's big windows, Tristan thought.

"Eric looks kind of crazed," Beth said, taking the seat next to Will and across from Ivy. Tristan was glad to see a pencil and notebook among Beth's clutter of dishes. Through her writing, he could communicate with all three of them at the same time. "What did he say?" she asked. "Is something wrong?"

Ivy shrugged. "He wants to talk to me later today."

"Why doesn't he talk to you now?" Will asked.

Good question, thought Tristan.

"He said he wants to see me alone." Ivy lowered her voice. "I'm not supposed to tell anyone."

Beth was watching Eric as he made his way toward the cafeteria doors. Her eyes narrowed.

I don't trust him, Tristan thought as clearly as possible. He had guessed right: Beth and he matched thoughts, and a moment later he was inside her mind. Then he felt her pull back.

"Don't be afraid, Beth," he said to her. "Don't throw me out. I need your help. Ivy needs your help."

Sighing, Beth picked up the pencil next to her notebook, and stirred her applesauce with it.

Will smiled and nudged her. "It'd be easier to eat with a spoon," he said.

Then Ivy's eyes widened a little. "Beth's glowing."

"Is it Tristan?" Will asked.

Beth dried her pencil and flipped open the notebook.

"Yes," she wrote.

Ivy frowned. "He can talk to me directly now. Why is he still communicating through you?"

Beth's fingers twitched, then she wrote quickly: "Because Beth still listens to me."

Will laughed out loud.

Beth's hand moved toward the page again. "I'm counting on Beth and Will to convince you—don't take chances with Eric!"

"Counting on me?" mumbled Will.

"It's too dangerous, Ivy," Beth scribbled. "It's a trap. Tell her, Will."

"I need to know the facts first," Will insisted.

"Eric asked me to meet him at five o'clock, by the river about a half mile below the double bridges," Ivy said.

Will nodded, tore the tip of a catsup packet, and spread its contents evenly on his hamburger. "Is that all?" he asked.

"He said to come alone and to look for him by an old car that's back a little from the river."

Will methodically opened a second catsup packet, then a mustard one. His slow and deliberate actions annoyed Tristan.

"Tell her, Will! Talk sense to her!" Beth wrote furiously.

But Will would not be hurried. "Eric could be setting a trap for you," he said to Ivy thoughtfully, "maybe a deadly one."

"Exactly," wrote Beth.

"Or," Will continued, "Eric could be telling the truth. He could be running scared and trying to give you some important information. I honestly don't know which it is."

"*Idiot!*" Beth wrote. "Don't do it, Ivy," she added out loud, her voice shaking. "That's me telling you, not Tristan."

Will turned to her. "What is it?" he asked. "What are you seeing?"

Tristan, inside her mind, was seeing it, too, and it shook him just as badly.

"It's the car," Beth said. "As soon as you mentioned it I could see it, an old car sinking slowly into the mud. Something terrible has happened there. There's a dark mist around it."

Will took Beth's trembling hand.

"The car's slipping into the ground like a coffin," she said. "Its hood is torn off. Its trunk . . . I can't see—there are lots of bushes and vines. There's a door partway open, blue, I think. Something's inside."

Beth's eyes were big and frightened, and a tear ran down her cheek. Will wiped it away gently, but another ran over his hand.

"The front seats are gone," she continued. "But I can see the back seat, and there's something . . ." She shook her head.

"Go on," Will urged softly.

"It's covered with a blanket. And there's an angel looking down on it. The angel is crying."

"What's under the blanket?" Ivy whispered.

"I can't see," Beth whispered back. "I can't see!"

Then her hand started scribbling: "I can see only what Beth sees. The blanket can't be lifted."

"Is the angel you, Tristan?" Ivy asked.

"No," Beth wrote. Then she grabbed Ivy's hand. "Something terrible is there. Don't go! I'm begging you, Ivy."

"Listen to her, Ivy!" Tristan said, but Beth's hand was shaking too hard to write it.

Ivy looked at Will.

"Beth has been right twice before," he said.

Ivy nodded, then sighed. "But what if Eric really has something important to tell me?"

"He'll find another way," Will reasoned. "If he really wants to tell you something, he'll figure out a way."

"I guess so," Ivy said, and Tristan sank down in relief.

Soon after that, he left the three of them. He heard Ivy ask mentally, "Where are you going?" But knowing she was in safe hands, he kept on. He had recovered from the exhaustion of time-traveling but wasn't sure how long his second wind would last. He wanted time to search Gregory's room while everyone was out of the house. If he could find Gregory's latest purchase of drugs, Ivy would have evidence for at least a drug charge.

Still, what she really needed was the jacket and cap, Tristan thought as he passed through the school door. The clothes might convince the police to reconsider Philip's story. A single piece of hair could establish the important link to Gregory.

Somebody must have found the clothes after they rolled off the motorcycle. Did that person know how important they were? Philip's story hadn't been released to the public, but it could have leaked out. Was there, Tristan wondered, an unidentified player in Gregory's game?

"But Ivy," Suzanne wailed, "we had plans to find the crystal slippers—the ruby shoes—the only pair of heels in all New England that are exactly right for my birthday party. And I've got only a week left to hunt!"

"I'm sorry," Ivy replied, reaching into her locker for another book. "I know I promised." She shifted the stack in her arms, clutching a note beneath the books. Three minutes before Suzanne had arrived, Ivy had opened her locker and found Tristan's picture gone. The note she grasped had been taped in its place.

"How about Wednesday?" Ivy proposed. "I have to work after school tomorrow, but we can shop till we drop on Wednesday and find you an incredible pair of shoes."

"By that time Gregory and I will have made up and be doing something again."

"Made up?" Ivy repeated. "What do you mean?"

Suzanne smiled. "It worked, Ivy, worked like a charm." With her back against the wall of lockers, Suzanne bent her knees and slowly slid down till her bottom touched the floor—no easy feat in tight jeans, Ivy thought. A group of guys down the hall admired her athletic ability.

"Since you wouldn't mention Jeff to him," Suzanne went on, "I did. I called Gregory Jeff."

"You called him Jeff? Did he notice?"

"Both times," Suzanne replied.

"Whew."

"Once when things were pretty hot and heavy."

"Suzanne!"

Suzanne threw back her head and laughed. It was a wild and infectious laugh, and people grinned as they passed her in the hall.

"So what did Gregory say? What did he do?" Ivy asked.

"He was unbelievably jealous," Suzanne said, her eyes flashing with excitement. "It's a wonder he didn't kill us both!"

"What do you mean?"

Suzanne slid closer to Ivy and bent her head, her

long, dark hair falling forward, like a curtain for telling secrets behind.

"The second time, we were in the back seat." Suzanne closed her eyes a moment, remembering. "His face went white, then the red started creeping up his neck. I swear I could feel a hundred and five degrees rushing through him. He pulled away from me and raised his hand. I thought he was going to hit me, and for a moment I was terrified."

She gazed into Ivy's eyes, her pupils large with excitement. Ivy could see that Suzanne might have been terrified then, but now found it thrilling and fun to talk about. Her friend was enjoying the memory the way someone delighted in a good scare at a spook house—but Gregory was no papier-mâché monster.

"Then he dropped his hand, called me a couple of names, got out of the back seat and into the front, and started driving like crazy. He opened all the windows and kept yelling back at me that I could get out. But of course he was driving so fast and weaving left and right, and I was trying to straighten myself up and kept slamming from one side of the car to the other. He'd watch me in the rearview mirror; sometimes he turned all the way around. It's a wonder he didn't kill us both."

Ivy stared at her friend in horror.

"Oh, come on, Ivy. In the end, when I had my right arm in the left arm of my vest and my hair flopped over my face, he slowed down, and both of us started laughing."

Ivy dropped her head in her hands.

"But when he took me home that night," Suzanne continued, "he said he didn't want to see me anymore. He said I make him lose control and do crazy things." She sounded pleased with herself, as if she had been given a huge compliment. "But he'll come around by next Saturday. He'll be at my party, you can bet on that."

"Suzanne, you're playing with fire," Ivy said.

Suzanne smiled.

"You and Gregory aren't good for each other," Ivy told her. "Look at you. You're both acting crazy."

Suzanne shrugged and laughed.

"You're acting like a fool!"

Suzanne blinked, stung by Ivy's criticism.

"Gregory has a terrible temper," Ivy went on. "Anything can happen. You don't know him the way I do."

"Oh, really?" Suzanne raised her eyebrows. "I think I know him pretty well."

"Suzanne—"

"And I can handle him—better than you can," she added, glancing sideways, her eyes gleaming. "So don't get your hopes up."

"What?"

"That's what this is all about, isn't it? Ever since you lost Tristan, you've been interested in Gregory. But he's mine, not yours, Ivy, and you're not going to get him away from me!"

Suzanne stood up quickly, brushed off the back of her jeans, and stalked down the hall.

Ivy leaned back against her locker. She knew it was pointless to call after Suzanne and thought about summoning Tristan, asking him to watch over her friend. Maybe Lacey could help them out. But that request would have to wait. Ivy had changed her plans for the afternoon, and if Tristan read her mind, he might try to stop her.

She unfolded the square of paper that had been taped in place of Tristan's picture. The note, signed with Eric's initials, was short and convincing:

"Come alone. Five o'clock. I know why you're dreaming what you're dreaming."

8

Ivy parked her car close to the train bridges. She was in the same clearing where Gregory had stopped months ago, the night Eric wanted to play chicken. She got out and walked the short distance to the double bridges. In the late-afternoon sun, the rails of the new bridge gleamed. Next to it stood the old bridge, a rusted orange fretwork reaching halfway across the river. Jagged fingers of metal and rotting wood reached back from the opposite bank of the river, but the two halves of the old bridge, like two groping hands, had lost touch.

When Ivy saw the parallel bridges clearly in the sunlight, when she saw the seven-foot gap between them and the long fall down to the water and rocks below, she realized the kind of risk Eric had taken when he pretended to leap from the new bridge. What went on inside Eric's head? she wondered.

Either he was totally insane or he just didn't care whether he lived or died.

Eric's Harley was not in sight, but there were plenty of trees and brush to hide it in. Ivy glanced around, then picked her way carefully down the steep bank next to the bridges, sliding part of the way until she reached a narrow path that ran along the river. She walked as quietly as possible, alert to every sound around her. When the trees rustled she looked up quickly, half expecting to see Eric and Gregory ready to swoop down on their prey.

"Get a grip, Ivy," she chided herself, but she continued to tread softly. If she could surprise Eric, she might see what he was up to before she walked into a trap.

Ivy glanced at her watch several times, and at five minutes past five she wondered if she had passed the car. But after a few more feet, something flashed in her eyes—sunlight glinting off metal. Fifteen feet ahead, she saw an overgrown path that led from the river to a metal heap.

Ivy worked her way into the brush, keeping herself hidden as she crept closer. Once she thought she heard something behind her, a soft crunch of leaves beneath someone's foot. She turned quickly. Nothing. Nothing but a few leaves drifting in the breeze.

Ivy pushed aside some long branches and took two steps forward, then drew in her breath sharply. The car was just as Beth had described it, its axles sunk into the earth, its rear buried beneath vines. The car's hood was ripped off, and its vinyl roof had decayed into papery black flakes. Its scarred doors shone blue—exactly as Beth had said.

The back door was open. Was there a blanket on the seat inside? Ivy wondered. What was under the blanket?

Again she heard rustling behind her and turned quickly around, searching the trees. Her eyes ached from focusing and refocusing on every shadow and flutter of leaf, searching for the shape of a person watching her. No one.

She glanced at her watch. Ten after five. Eric wouldn't have given up on her this soon, she thought. Either he's late or he's waiting for me to make the first move. Well, two can play the waiting game, Ivy reasoned, and crouched down quietly.

A few minutes later her legs began to ache with the tension of holding still. She rubbed them and looked at her watch again: quarter after. She waited five more minutes. Maybe Eric has lost his nerve, she thought.

Ivy stood up slowly, but something kept her from moving any further. She heard Beth's warning as if her friend were standing next to her, whispering in her ear.

"Angels, help me," Ivy prayed. Part of her wanted to find out what was in the car. But part of her wanted to run away. "Angels, are you there? Tristan, I need you. I need you now!"

She walked tentatively toward the car. When she reached the clearing she paused for just a moment, waiting to see if anyone had followed. Then she bent down and looked in the back seat.

Ivy blinked, unsure for a moment that what she saw was real—not another nightmare, not one more of Eric's jokes. Then she screamed, screamed until her throat was raw. She knew without touching him—he was too pale, too still, his blue eyes open and staring at nothing—that Eric was dead.

Ivy jumped when someone touched her from behind. She started screaming again. Arms wrapped around her, pulling her back, holding her tight. She thought she'd shriek her brains out. He didn't try to stop her, just held her till she went limp, her whole body sagging against him. His face brushed hers.

"Will," she said. She could feel his body shaking.

He turned her toward him and held her face against his chest, his hand shielding her eyes. But in her mind Ivy could still see Eric staring upward, his eyes wide, as if he were quietly amazed by what had happened.

Will shifted his weight, and Ivy knew he was looking over her shoulder at Eric. "I—I don't see any signs of trouble," he said. "No bruising. No blood."

Ivy's stomach suddenly rose up against her ribs. She gritted her teeth and forced it back down. "Maybe drugs," she said. "An overdose."

Will nodded. His breath was short and quick against her cheek. "We have to call the police."

Then Ivy pulled away from him. She bent down and forced herself to look long and hard at Eric. She should memorize the scene, she thought. She should collect clues. What had happened to him could be a warning to her. But as she looked at Eric all she felt was the loss; all she could see was a wasted life.

Ivy reached into the car. Will caught her hand. "Don't. Don't touch him," he said. "Leave his body just as it is so that the police can examine it."

Ivy nodded, then picked up an old blanket from the car floor and gently laid it on top of Eric. "Angels—" she began, but she did not know what to ask for. "Help him," she said, and left the prayer at that. As she walked away she knew that a merciful angel of the dead was looking down on Eric, weeping—just as Beth had said.

"Despite what you say, Lacey, I'm glad I missed my own funeral," Tristan observed as the mourners gathered at Eric's graveside. Some of them stood solitary and stiff as soldiers; others leaned against each other for support and comfort.

Friday had dawned pale and drizzly. Several people raised umbrellas now, like bright nylon flowers blooming against the gray stones and misty trees. Ivy and Beth stood on either side of Will, bareheaded, letting the rain and tears run together. Suzanne stood with one arm around Gregory, staring down at the bristling grass.

Three times in five months the four of them had stood together at Riverstone Rise, and still the police asked only routine questions about the deaths.

"No luck?" Lacey called down from her perch in a tree.

Tristan grunted. "Gregory's built a wall around himself," he replied, and walked in frustrated circles around the elm. He had tried several times during the church service to get inside Gregory's head. "Sometimes I think that the moment I approach him, he senses me. I think he knows something's up as soon as I get near him."

"Could be," Lacey said. Materializing her fingers, she swung from a branch, dropping down neatly beside him. "In angel matters, you're not exactly a smooth operator."

"What do you mean?"

"Well, let's put it this way. If you were stealing TVs instead of thoughts," she told him, "you'd have been caught by a half-deaf, mostly blind, fifteen-year-old dog three robberies ago."

Tristan was stung. "Well, give me two years to procrastinate," he retorted, "excuse me, I meant two years to *practice*, and I'll be as good as you."

"Maybe," Lacey said, then added with a smile, "I tried getting inside him, too. Impossible."

Tristan studied Gregory's face. He gave away nothing, his mouth an even line, his eyes focused straight ahead.

"You know," Lacey said, materializing the palm

of her hand and holding it up to catch raindrops, "Gregory doesn't have to be responsible for *everything* bad that happens. You saw the report. The police found no signs of a struggle."

The coroner had listed Eric's death as a drug overdose. Eric's parents insisted it was an accident. At school it was rumored to be suicide. Tristan believed it was murder.

"The report doesn't prove anything," he argued, pacing back and forth. "Gregory didn't have to force-feed Eric. He could have bought him a heavy dose without telling him how powerful it was. He could have waited till Eric was too high to know better, then given him more. The reason the police aren't thinking murder, Lacey, is because they have no motive for it."

"And you do."

"Eric was ready to talk. He was ready to tell Ivy something."

"Aha! Then the chick was right," Lacey needled him.

"She was right," he admitted, though he was still angry with Ivy for trying to meet with Eric on Monday afternoon. She had called out to him at the very last minute, when it would have been too late for him to save her. Rushing to her side, Tristan had found her walking with Will away from the dangerous site. Will said he had followed Ivy that afternoon on a sudden hunch.

"Are you still feeling left out?" Lacey asked.

He didn't reply.

"Tristan, when is it going to sink in? We're *dead*," Lacey said. "And that's what happens when you're dead. People forget to invite you along."

Tristan kept his eyes on Ivy. He wanted to be next to her, holding her hand.

"We're here to give a hand when we can and then let go," Lacey told him. "We help, and then it's bye-bye." She waved both hands at him.

"Like I said before, Lacey, I hope you fall in love one day. I hope that before your mission's done, some guy teaches you how miserable it feels to love somebody and watch him reach out for someone else."

Lacey stepped back.

"I hope you learn what it's like to say good-bye to someone you love more than that person will ever guess."

She turned her face away from him. "You just might get your wish," she said.

He glanced at her, surprised by her tone of voice. He didn't usually have to worry about hurting Lacey's feelings. "Did I miss something?" he asked.

She shook her head.

"What?" he asked. "What is it?" He reached for her face.

Lacey pulled away from him.

"You're missing the final prayer," she said. "We should pray with everyone else for Eric." Lacey folded her hands and looked extremely angelic.

Tristan sighed. "You pray in my place," he said.

"I don't have many good feelings toward Eric."

"All the more reason to pray," she replied. "If he doesn't rest in peace, he may be hanging out with us."

"Angels, take care of him. Let him rest in peace," Ivy prayed. "Help Eric's family," she said silently, and gazed back at Christine, Eric's older sister. She stood with her parents and brothers on the other side of the casket.

Several times during the service, Ivy had caught Christine looking at her. When their eyes met, the girl's mouth trembled a little, then became a long, soft line. Christine had Eric's pale blond hair and porcelain skin, but her eyes were a vibrant blue. She was beautiful—an uncomfortable reminder of what Eric might have been like if drugs and alcohol had not wasted his body and mind.

"Angels, take care of him," Ivy prayed again.

The minister concluded the service, and everyone turned away at the same time. Gregory's fingers brushed Ivy's. His hand was as cold as ice. She remembered how cold it had felt the evening the police told them of Caroline's death.

"How are you doing?" she asked.

He slipped his hand through hers and held her fingers tightly. The night Caroline had died, when he had done the very same thing, she had believed that he was finally reaching out to her.

"I'm okay," he said. "How about you?"

"Glad it's over," she answered honestly.

He studied her face, every centimeter of it. She felt trapped, anchored by his hand, his eyes invading her, reading her thoughts.

"I'm sorry, Gregory. You and Eric were friends for so long," she said. "I know this is much harder for you than for any of the rest of us."

Gregory continued to gaze at her.

"You tried to help him, Gregory. You did all you could for him," Ivy said. "We both know that."

Gregory bowed his head, moving his face close to hers. Ivy's skin tingled. To someone who didn't know better, to Andrew and Maggie watching them from a distance, it would look like a moment of shared sorrow. But to Ivy it felt like the movement of an animal she didn't trust, a dog that didn't bite but intimidated by moving its teeth very close to her bare skin.

"Gregory!"

He was so focused on Ivy that he jumped when Suzanne rested her hand on the back of his neck. Ivy stepped back quickly, and Gregory let go of her.

He's as edgy as I am, Ivy thought as she watched Suzanne and Gregory make their way to the cars parked along the cemetery road. Beth and Will started off, and Ivy followed slowly behind them. Out of the corner of her eye she saw Eric's sister walking toward her with long strides.

Ivy had told the police that she and Will were on an after-school hike when they came upon Eric in the car. After Dr. and Mrs. Ghent learned of Eric's death, they had telephoned her to discuss the story she'd given to the police and probe for more details. Now she steeled herself for another round of questioning.

"You're Ivy Lyons, aren't you?" the girl asked. Her cheeks were smooth and pink, her thick hair shining in the rain. It was startling to be confronted by such a healthy version of Eric.

"Yes," Ivy replied. "I'm sorry, Christine. I'm really sorry for you and your family."

The girl acknowledged Ivy's sympathy with a nod. "You—you must have been close to Eric," she said.

"Excuse me?"

"I figured you were special to him."

Ivy looked at her, mystified.

"Because of what he left. When—when Eric and I were younger," Christine began, her voice shaking a little, "we used to leave messages for each other in a secret place in the attic. We put them in an old cardboard box. On the box we wrote 'Beware! Frogs! Do Not Open!'"

Christine laughed, then tears sprang into the corners of her eyes. Ivy waited patiently, wondering where this conversation was leading.

"When I came home for this—for his funeral, I looked in our box, just on a whim," Christine continued, "not expecting to find anything—we hadn't used it for years. But I found a note to me. And this."

She pulled a gray envelope from her purse. "The note said, 'If anything happens to me, give this to Ivy Lyons.'"

Ivy's eyes widened.

"You weren't expecting it," Christine observed. "You don't know what's in it."

"No," Ivy said, then took the sealed envelope in her hand. She could feel a small, stiff wad inside, as if a hard object had been wrapped in padding. The outside of the envelope intrigued Ivy even more. Eric's name and address had been typed neatly onto it and her own name scribbled in big letters across it. The return-address sticker bore the name and address of Caroline Baines.

"Oh, that," Christine said when Ivy fingered it. "It's probably just an old envelope Eric had lying around."

But it wasn't just an old envelope. Ivy checked the postmark: May 28, Philip's birthday. The day Caroline died.

"Maybe you didn't know," Christine continued. "Eric was very close to Caroline. She was a second mother to him."

Ivy looked up, surprised. "She was?"

"From the time he was a kid, Eric and my mother never got along," Christine explained. "I'm six years older, and I took care of him sometimes when my mother worked long days in New York. But usually he was at the Baines house, and Caroline became closer to him than any of us. Even after she divorced and Gregory didn't live with her, Eric would often go see her."

"I didn't know that," Ivy said.

"Are you going to open it?" Christine asked, looking at the envelope curiously.

Ivy tore off one corner and slit the envelope with her finger. "If it's a personal note," she warned Christine, "I might not show it to you."

Christine nodded.

But there was no note, just dry tissue wrapped around the hard object. Ivy tore at it and pulled out a key. It was about two inches long. One end was oval, with a lacy design cut into the metal. The other end, which would fit into a lock, was a simple hollow cylinder with two small teeth at the tip.

"Do you know what it's for?" Christine asked.

"No," Ivy replied. "And there isn't a note."

Christine bit her lip, then said, "Well, maybe it was an accident after all." Ivy could hear the hope in her voice. "I mean, if Eric planned to kill himself, he would have left a note explaining this—wouldn't he?"

Unless he was murdered before he got a chance, Ivy thought, but she nodded in agreement with Christine.

"Eric didn't commit suicide," Ivy said in a firm voice. Then she saw the gratitude in Christine's eyes and blushed. If Christine only knew, Ivy thought, that I might have been the cause of her brother's death.

Ivy dropped the key into the envelope, tucked the flap in, and folded the envelope in half. Slipping it in her raincoat pocket, she told Christine she'd let her know if she figured out what the key was for.

Christine thanked Ivy for being a good friend to Eric, which sent more color rushing into Ivy's cheeks.

Her face was still warm when she joined Will and Beth, who had been watching her from twenty feet away, huddled together under an umbrella.

"What did she say to you?" Will asked, pulling Ivy under the umbrella with them.

"She—uh—thanked me for being Eric's good friend."

"Oh, boy," Beth said softly.

"Is that all?" Will asked.

It was a question Ivy had come to expect from Gregory when he was pumping her for information.

"You talked pretty long," Will observed. "Is that all she said?"

"Yes," Ivy lied.

Will's eyes dropped down to the pocket where she had shoved the envelope. He must have seen the exchange, and certainly he could see the edge of the envelope now, but he didn't question her further.

They had been excused from school that day, and the three of them drove quietly to Celentano's for a late lunch. As they pored over their menus Ivy wondered what Will was thinking and if he was suspicious of Gregory. At the police station on Monday, Will had let her do the talking, then echoed her story, neither of them mentioning Eric's request for a secret meeting. Now Ivy wanted to tell Will everything. If she looked too long into his eyes, she would.

"So how are you all doing?" Pat Celentano said, coming to take their order. Most of the lunchtime customers had left the the pizza shop, and the owner was speaking in a quieter voice than usual. "Rough morning for you."

She took their order, then set an extra basket of pencils and crayons on the paper tablecloth.

Will, who already had several tablecloth drawings hanging on Celentano's walls, began sketching immediately. Ivy doodled. Beth made long chains of rhyming words, murmuring to herself as the lists grew. "Sorry," she said when one of her chains ran into Will's drawing.

He was writing and illustrating knock-knock jokes. Beth and Ivy leaned over to read them, and started laughing together softly. Will sketched them in their Old West photo costumes. "Virginia City Sweethearts," he titled it.

Beth pointed to the drawing. "I think you missed a few curves," she said. "Ivy's dress was a lot tighter than that. Of course, not as tight as your cowboy pants."

Ivy smiled, remembering the voice that had confused them all that day, a voice coming out of nowhere—Lacey having a little fun.

"Love those buns!" Ivy and Beth said at the same time, and this time they laughed out loud.

With the sudden laughter came tears. Ivy covered her face with one hand.

Will and Beth sat silently and let her cry it out,

then Will gently placed her hand on the table and began to trace it. Over and over the pencil ran along the sides of her fingers, the smooth touch of it soothing her. Then Will positioned his hand on the paper at an angle against hers and traced it too.

When he lifted their hands, Ivy gazed down at the design. "Wings," she said, smiling a little. "A butterfly, or an angel."

He let go of her hand. Ivy longed to move close to Will and rest against him. She wanted to tell him everything she knew and ask his help. But she knew she couldn't put him in danger. Because of her, one guy she had loved with all her heart had already been murdered. She wasn't going to let it happen to the— Ivy caught herself. To the other guy she . . . loved?

9

When Ivy was dropped off later that afternoon, she never went into the house. With Eric's envelope still in her pocket, she climbed into her own car and started driving. After an hour of going nowhere, taking back roads that followed the river north, then crossing over, winding her way south, and crossing again into town, she stopped at the park at the end of Main Street.

The rain had finally ended, and the empty park was drenched with late-afternoon color, the sun slanting through blue-black clouds and turning the grass a brilliant green. Ivy sat alone in the wooden pavilion, remembering the day of the arts festival. Gregory had watched her from one side of the lawn, Will from the other. But it was Tristan's presence she had felt when she played. Was he there? When she played the

"Moonlight Sonata," did he know it was for him?

"I was there. I knew it."

Ivy gazed down at her shimmering hands and smiled. "Tristan," she said softly.

"Ivy." His voice was like light inside her. "Ivy, what were you running from?"

The question caught her off guard. "What?"

"What were you driving away from?" Tristan asked.

"I was just driving."

"You were upset," he said.

"I was trying to think, that's all. But I couldn't," she confessed.

"What couldn't you think about?"

"You." Ivy ran her hand up and down the smooth, damp wood of the railing she sat on. "You died because of me. I knew it, but I didn't face it, not until now, when I realized that Eric might have died because of me. Not until I thought about what could happen to Will if he learns what's going on."

"Will's going to find out one way or the other," Tristan told her.

"We can't let him!" Ivy said. "We can't endanger him."

"If you feel that way," Tristan observed dryly, "you shouldn't have left your coat with him at the table."

Ivy reached quickly into her pocket. The envelope was still there, folded in half, but when she pulled it out she saw that the flap was no longer tucked in.

"He looked as soon as you and Beth left him alone."

Ivy closed her eyes for a moment, feeling betrayed. "I guess—I guess I would have been curious, too," she said lamely.

"What do you think the key goes to?" Tristan asked.

Ivy flipped the envelope over in her hands. "Some kind of small box or cupboard. At Caroline's house," she added, looking at the address. "Can you get inside?"

"Easily, and I can materialize my fingers to undo the latch to let you in," he told her. "Bring the key, and we'll find what Eric wanted you to find. But not today, okay?"

Ivy heard the strain in his voice. "Is something wrong?"

"I'm tired. Real tired."

"The darkness," she whispered in a frightened voice. Tristan had said there would be a time when he wouldn't return from the darkness.

"It's okay," he assured her. "I just need rest. You're keeping me busy, you know." He laughed.

It's because of me, Ivy thought. He died because of me, and now—

"Ivy, no. You can't think that way," he said.

"But I do think that way," she argued. "I was the one who was supposed to die. If it weren't for me—"

"If it weren't for you, I would never have known how it is to love someone," he told her. "If it weren't for you, I would never have kissed a mouth so sweet."

Ivy longed to kiss him now. "Tristan," she said, trembling with the sudden idea, "if I died, I could be with you."

He was silent. She could feel the confusion of thoughts, all the emotions tossing within him, within her.

"I could be with you forever," she told him.

"No."

"Yes!"

"That's not how it's supposed to be," he said. "We both know that."

Ivy got up and walked around the pavilion. His presence within her was stronger than the autumn day outside of her. When he was with her, the smell of soaked earth, the ribbons of emerald grass, and the first scarlet leaves all paled like objects on the edge of her vision.

"I wouldn't have been sent back to help you," Tristan continued. "I wouldn't have been made an angel if it weren't important that you live. Ivy, I want you to be mine"—she could hear the pain in his voice—"but you're not."

"I am!" she cried out loud.

"We're on different sides of a river," he said, "and it's a river that neither of us can cross. You were meant for somebody else."

"I was meant for *you,*" she insisted.

"Hush."

"I don't want to lose you, Tristan!"

"Shhh. Shhh," he soothed. "Listen, Ivy, I'm going

116

to be in the darkness soon, and it may be a while before I reach you again."

Ivy paced around.

"Stay still. I'm going outside of you, so you won't be able to hear me," he told her. "Stay still."

Then all was silent. Ivy stood motionless, wondering. The air around her began to shimmer with gold. She felt hands touching her, gentle hands cradling her face, lifting her chin. He kissed her. His lips touched hers, actually touched hers with a kiss long and unbearably tender. "Ivy"—she couldn't hear him, but she felt her name whispered by him against her cheek. "Ivy." Then he was gone.

10

Ivy hung a long dangle earring on each ear, wiped away a smudge of mascara beneath one eye, then took a step back from the mirror, surveying herself.

"You look hot."

She glanced at Philip's reflection in the mirror and burst out laughing. "You didn't pick up *that* expression from Andrew. And how do you know what hot looks like, anyway?"

"I taught him."

Ivy spun around. Gregory stood in the entrance to her bedroom, leaning casually against the door frame. Since Eric's death nearly a week before, Ivy had felt Gregory's presence following her like a dark angel.

"And you do look hot," he added, his eyes moving down her slowly.

Maybe I should have chosen a skirt that's not so short, Ivy thought, or a top that isn't scooped so low.

But she was determined to show the others at Suzanne's birthday party that she wasn't a depressed girl ready to choose the suicidal path everyone thought Eric had taken. Suzanne was still having her party, though it was the day after the funeral. Ivy had encouraged her, telling Suzanne it would be good for everyone—the kids from school needed to come together now.

"It's the colors. They make you hot," Philip said to Ivy, anxious to sound as if he knew what he was talking about.

Ivy glanced at Gregory. "Good job, teach."

Gregory laughed. "I did my best," he said, then he held up his car keys and rattled them.

Ivy grabbed her own keys and purse.

"Ivy, this is silly," Gregory said. "Why are we going to the same place and taking two cars?"

They had already argued about her decision during dinner. "I told you, I'll probably leave before you do." She picked up a wrapped gift for Suzanne and turned out the lamp on her dressing table. "You're dating the hostess—everyone will probably leave before you do."

Gregory smiled slightly and shrugged. "Maybe, but if you want to leave, there will be lots of guys there glad to give you a ride home."

"Because you look hot," Philip said. "Because you—"

"Thank you, Philip."

Gregory winked at her brother. Philip jumped off her bed, using her scarf as a parachute, and scooted through the bathroom that joined his room with hers.

Gregory continued to lean against Ivy's door. "Is my

driving that bad?" he asked, stretching one arm across the doorway, blocking her exit. "If I didn't know better, I'd think you were afraid to drive with me."

"I'm not," Ivy said firmly.

"Maybe you're afraid of being alone with me."

"Oh, come on," Ivy said, walking briskly toward him and pulling his arm down. She turned him around by the shoulders and gave him a push. "Let's get going or we'll be late. I hope your Beamer has gas."

Gregory reached back for her hand and pulled her close to him, too close. Ivy's heart was beating fast as they moved down the stairs—she really didn't want to ride alone with him. She wished he weren't so attentive when she got into his car. The constant small and needless touches jangled her nerves. He kept looking at her as he drove slowly down the driveway.

When they stopped at the bottom of the ridge, Gregory said, "Let's not go to Suzanne's."

"What?" Ivy exclaimed. She tried to cover her growing apprehension with a show of disbelief and amazement. "Suzanne and I have been friends since we were seven, and you think I'm skipping her seventeenth-birthday party? Drive!" she commanded. "To Lantern Road. Or I'm getting out."

Gregory rested his hand on her leg and drove to Suzanne's house. Fifteen minutes later, when Suzanne answered the door, she did not appear overly delighted to see Gregory and Ivy together.

"He insisted on driving me," Ivy said. "He'll do anything to make you jealous, Suzanne."

Gregory shot her a look, but Suzanne laughed, her face brightening.

"You look gorgeous," Ivy told her friend, and gave her a hug. Ivy felt a moment of hesitation, then Suzanne hugged her back.

"Where do I stash this present?" Ivy asked as a large group of kids who had crammed themselves into a Jeep came in behind them.

"End of the hall," Suzanne said, pointing to a table with an impressive pile of boxes. Ivy headed quickly in that direction, glad to be away from Gregory. The Goldsteins' long center hallway led to a family room that ran along the back of the house, its floor-to-ceiling windows facing a porch and the back lawn, which sloped down gently to a pond. It was a warm September night, and the party had spread out from the large room to the porch and lawn below.

Walking out on the porch, Ivy saw Beth sitting in the swing at one end, deep in conversation with two cheerleaders. The two girls were talking excitedly at the same time, and Beth's head went back and forth as if she were watching a tennis match.

Out of the corner of her eye she caught sight of Will, sitting on the wide porch steps next to a girl with auburn hair, the girl he had been with six weeks ago when Ivy ran into him at the mall. Now, *she* was hot.

"Wish I could read minds," Gregory said, touching a cold glass to Ivy's arm.

It seemed impossible to move out from under his shadow.

"What are you doing—putting a hex on that girl?" he asked.

Ivy shook her head. "I was just thinking, thinking that when it comes to hot, that girl is *it*."

Gregory watched Will's companion for a moment, then shrugged. "Some girls look hot on the outside, but it's just a tease. Other girls, they put you off, play hard to get, act like ice queens"—he looked at her with laughing eyes—"but they're running hot." He moved closer to her. "Real hot," he whispered.

Ivy flashed him an innocent smile. "Like Philip, I can always learn something from you."

Gregory laughed. "Did you get a drink?" he asked, offering with his left hand a plastic cup.

"I'm not thirsty," Ivy said. "Thanks anyway."

"But I got this for you. I saw you standing over here, checking out Will—"

"I wasn't checking out Will," she protested.

"Okay, checking out the redhead, then—her name's Samantha—and I thought you could use something to cool off."

"Thanks." Ivy reached for the cup in his right hand.

Was it her imagination, or did Gregory move it away from her? Ivy had remembered Lacey's warning and didn't want to drink from the cup he was offering. But he insisted that she take it, and she finally did. "Thanks. I'll be seeing you around," Ivy told him airily.

"Where are you going?"

"Cruising," she replied. "I didn't wear this short skirt for nothing."

"Can I come?"

"Of course not." She laughed up at him as if he had said something he knew was silly. Inside she was so tense, her stomach hurt when she breathed. "How can I check out guys with you around?"

To her relief, Gregory didn't follow her. Ivy dumped her soda in the garden as soon as he was out of sight. Working her way around the party, she smiled and listened to any guy who looked as if he needed an audience, while always steering clear of Gregory. She circled around Will, too, and didn't see either of them again until Suzanne blew out the candles on her cake.

When everyone had gathered for the song and cake-cutting, Suzanne wanted Ivy to stand on one side of her and Gregory on the other. Mrs. Goldstein, who trusted Suzanne enough to watch the party from an upstairs window—without her glasses, she told them—made an entrance with the cake and took what seemed like a hundred pictures of Suzanne, Ivy, and Gregory.

"Now each with your arm around her," Mrs. Goldstein directed them.

Ivy slipped her arm around Suzanne's back.

"Beautiful! You're all beautiful!" *Flash*.

"Let me get another shot," Mrs Goldstein said, then shook the camera and muttered to it. "Don't move."

They didn't, not from the front, but behind Suzanne's back, Gregory began to run a finger up and down Ivy's arm. Then he used two fingers, stroking her in a slow, caressing motion. Ivy wanted to scream. She wanted to slap him away.

"Smile," Mrs. Goldstein said. *Flash.*

"And one more. Ivy—"

She forced a smile. *Flash.*

Ivy tried not to pull away too quickly from Gregory. She remembered Philip's dream about the train—the silver snake—that wanted to swallow her up. He's always watching, Philip had said, and he smells it when you're afraid.

Suzanne began cutting the cake, and Ivy handed it out. When she gave Gregory a piece, he touched her lightly on the wrist and wouldn't take the cake till she met his gaze.

Will was next in line. "We keep missing each other," he said to Ivy.

She was about to tell him to take two plates and meet her by the pond in ten minutes, but then she saw Samantha standing right behind him.

"Big party," Ivy said.

Fifteen minutes later Ivy was sitting alone on a bench about twenty feet away from the pond, eating her cake and watching Peppermint, Suzanne's Pomeranian. The little dog, who was regularly shampooed and conditioned, and let outdoors only on a leash, had escaped that night and was happily digging holes in the muddy bank. Then she waded into the pond and began to do the doggy paddle.

Some girls and guys standing by the pond called to the dog, trying to get her to fetch sticks, but Peppermint was as headstrong as her mistress. Then

Ivy called softly. Too late she realized her mistake. Peppermint knew Ivy. Peppermint liked Ivy. Peppermint loved cake. She came running on her short little legs, made a flying leap for Ivy's lap, then scrambled up the rest of the way with her muddy back feet. She put her slimy front paws on Ivy's chest so she could stand up and lick her face, then dropped down in Ivy's lap and shook out her thick coat full of water.

"Pep! Hey!" Ivy wiped her face, then shook her own mane hair. The dog saw her chance and gulped the rest of Ivy's cake. "Pep, you muddy pig!"

Ivy heard a burst of laughter next to her. Will dropped down on the bench beside her. "I'm sorry Mrs. Goldstein wasn't here with her camera," he said.

"And I'm sorry you didn't call Peppermint first," Ivy replied.

He couldn't stop laughing. "I'll get some towels," he sputtered, "for both of you."

He was quick about it and brought back a pile of wet and dry cloths. Sitting on the bench next to her, Will cleaned the dog while Ivy tried unsuccessfully to remove the mud from her skirt and top.

"Maybe we should just dump you in the pond and make you all one color," Will said to Ivy.

"Great idea. Why don't you go see how deep it is for me?"

He grinned at her, then reached over with a clean cloth and wiped her cheek close to her ear. "It's in your hair too," he said.

She felt his fingers pulling gently on her hair, trying to get out the mud. She held still. When he let go of the strands, something inside her floated upward, wanting to be touched again.

Ivy looked down quickly at her skirt and ferociously attacked a mud stain. Then Will set Peppermint on the ground between them. The clean dog wagged its little tail at him. "I bet you wish you were a puppy like me."

Ivy and Will turned at the same time and bent down to the dog, bumping their heads together.

"Ow!"

Will started laughing again. They looked in each other's eyes, laughing at themselves, and didn't see if Peppermint's mouth moved when she "spoke" a second time.

"If you were a pup like me, Will, you could jump into Ivy's arms."

Ivy thought she recognized the voice and glanced around for a suspicious purple shimmer.

"You could put your head in Ivy's lap and be cuddled. I know that's what you'd like."

Ivy sneaked a peek at Will, embarrassed, but he didn't look at all sheepish. He was staring at the dog, his mouth drawn up in a little smile. "You can put words in a dog's mouth, angel," he said, "but not in mine."

"You're no fun! Even if you do have nice buns," Lacey added.

"I thought they were *great* buns," Will said.

Lacey laughed. Ivy spotted her then, right behind

them. Apparently she could throw her voice. Now the soft purple shine moved around in front of them.

"Her name's Lacey," Ivy told Will.

"I'm disappointed in you two," Lacey said. "I keep waiting for you to get things going, but you just tippy-toe around each other. As a romance, you get two thumbs down. I'm going to hang out with the kids by the pond."

Will shrugged. "Have a good time."

"Something tells me Peppermint won't be the only one taking a swim tonight," Ivy remarked under her breath.

The purple mist drifted back to them. "It's amazing how much we think alike, chick," Lacey said. "But the fact is, Tristan is still in the darkness, so I'll probably behave myself tonight. Without him around to fuss at me, it's not as much fun."

Ivy smiled a little.

"See, I miss him, too," Lacey said. For a moment her voice sounded different to Ivy, girlish and wistful. Then the tone became theatrical again: "Whoops, here she comes. Warning, ten feet behind you—chick with a capital C. I'm all gone, boys and girls."

But Lacey didn't leave immediately. "Mommy, I went swimming! I had so much fun!" Peppermint "said" in a voice loud enough for Suzanne to hear.

The purple shimmer slipped away as Suzanne came around to the front of the bench.

"Pep! Oh, Pep!" She felt the dog's wet fur. "You bad girl. I'm going to put you in your kennel."

127

Then she saw Ivy's mud-splattered skirt and top. "Ivy!"

"You going to put me in the kennel, too?" Ivy asked. Will laughed.

Suzanne shook her head. "I'm so sorry. Bad girl!"

Peppermint lowered her head contritely, until Suzanne turned to Ivy. Then her head popped up, and her tail wagged again.

"It's my fault," Ivy said. "I called Peppermint while she was swimming. It's no big deal—all I need is a little soap."

"I'll get it for you," Suzanne said.

"No, it's okay," Ivy replied, smiling. "I know where it is." She stood up.

"If you want to throw your clothes in the wash," Suzanne told her, "wear something of mine. You know which is the clean stuff."

"Whatever isn't on the floor," they both said at the same time, and laughed.

Ivy started toward the house and heard Suzanne ask Will how he made that dog voice. She was still smiling to herself when she entered the house. Then she hurried down the hall, glancing around for Gregory, hoping he didn't see her heading upstairs.

Ivy relaxed when she reached Suzanne's bedroom, a room she had spent countless hours in, gossiping, reading magazines, trying on makeup. The large, square room was furnished in dark polished wood and carpeted wall to wall in a pure, plush white. Suzanne and Ivy always joked that the best way to keep the carpet clean was to walk on her clothes. But that day Ivy removed her shoes. The room was picked up, with the green silk coverlet pulled smooth on the bed and just one filmy blouse tossed aside. Ivy took off her stained shirt, slipped on the blouse without buttoning it, and headed for Suzanne's bathroom.

The soap worked well on her knit top. She squeezed the top out in a towel, then hung it on a hanger. Having rigged up the hair dryer as she had seen Suzanne do, she turned it on to dry the knit while she worked on her skirt. Ivy was standing close to sink, pulling up her pale denim skirt and scrubbing it hard, when she felt the hot air on her back and her hair and blouse blow loose. She glanced up quickly.

In the mirror she saw Gregory, aiming the hair dryer at her and laughing.

Ivy wrapped the open blouse around her as if it were a coat. "It's the top that needs drying, not me," she said crisply.

Gregory laughed, flicked off the dryer and dropped it, letting it dangle from its electric cord.

"I'm losing patience," he said.

Ivy stared at him wide-eyed.

"I'm getting tired of chasing you," he said.

She bit her lip. "I don't know why you keep trying."

He tilted back his head, studying her as if he were making some kind of decision. He moved close to her. She could smell the alcohol on his breath. "Liar," he whispered in her ear. "Every guy out there would be chasing you if they thought they had a chance."

Ivy's mind raced. How much had Gregory drunk? What kind of game was he playing?

His arms encircled her. Ivy fought the panic that was growing inside her. She could not get away from him, so she put her arms around him lightly, trying to draw him out of the secluded bathroom. She had left the bedroom door open, and if she made it to where they could be seen and heard—

He moved easily with her into the bedroom. Then she saw that the door to the hall had been closed. He started pushing her toward the bed.

He can't kill me, not here, she thought as she was pushed back. It'd be too easy to trace him. She stepped back again. His fingerprints are on the hair dryer and the door, she reminded herself, stepping back and back. And someone could walk in at any moment, she told herself. He moved with her, so close she couldn't see his face.

Ivy tumbled onto the bed and stared up at him. Gregory's eyes were like hot gray coals. Color crept high in his cheeks. He's too smart to pull a gun, she thought. He'll jam a capsule down my throat.

Then Gregory was on top of her. Ivy struggled against him. Gregory laughed at her efforts as she squirmed beneath him, then he groaned softly. "I love you," he said.

Ivy held still, and he lifted his head, staring down at her, his eyes burning with a strange light. "I want you. I've wanted you for a long time."

Was this some kind of terrible joke?

"You know things about me," Gregory said softly, "but you're in love with me, aren't you, Ivy? You would never do anything to hurt me."

Was his ego that big? Was he that crazy? No, she thought, he's warning me.

He laid his hand on her neck. He stroked her throat with his thumb, then pressed it against her pulse. A smile spread across his face. "What did I tell you? Running hot and fast," he said. Then he removed his hand from her throat and slowly traced the edge of her unbuttoned shirt. Ivy's skin crawled.

"Goose bumps." He seemed pleased. "If a month from now I can't give you goose bumps with my touch, if you don't get hot when we kiss, I'll know you don't feel the same way you do now."

He really believed it!

"And that would be too bad," he said, still tracing her shirt with his finger. "I'd have to figure out what to do with you then." He leaned on her heavily and pressed his mouth against hers.

Play along, Ivy thought. Play to stay alive. Angels, where are you? She kissed him back, though everything inside her rose up in protest. She kissed him again. Oh, angels, help me! Gregory's kisses grew more passionate, more insistent.

She pushed against him, catching him by surprise. Shoving him away, she rolled off the bed. She could not hold it back—Ivy threw up on the rug.

When she stopped retching, she turned to look at Gregory, wiping her mouth with one hand, steadying herself against a chair with the other. She saw an entirely different expression on his face. He knew now. The curtain had been lifted, and there was no more pretending. He had seen exactly what she thought of him. His eyes showed what he now thought about her.

Before either of them could say anything, the bedroom door swung open. Suzanne stood in the doorway. "I noticed both of you were missing," she began, and gazed past them at the rumpled bed. Then she looked at the mess on the floor. "Oh, God!"

Gregory was ready for her. "Ivy's had too much to drink," he said.

"I haven't. I haven't had a thing!" Ivy said quickly.

"She can't tolerate alcohol," Gregory said, walking toward Suzanne, reaching out toward her.

Ivy moved with him. "Suzanne, please, listen to me."

"I was worried about her and—"

"I just talked to you," Ivy reminded Suzanne. "I just talked to you—did I seem drunk?"

But Suzanne looked at her blankly.

"Answer me!" Ivy demanded. The faraway look in Suzanne's eyes scared her. Her friend's mind had already been poisoned by what she saw.

"Nice blouse," Suzanne remarked. "Couldn't find the buttons?"

Ivy pulled it closed.

"I came up to see if she was all right," Gregory continued, "and she, you know—" He paused as if he were embarrassed. "She came on to me. I guess that doesn't really surprise you."

"It doesn't," Suzanne replied in a cool, distant voice.

"Suzanne," Ivy pleaded, "listen to me. We've been friends all this time and you trusted me—"

"This time she came on strong," Gregory said. He frowned. "I guess it was the booze."

This time? Ivy thought. "I swear to you, Suzanne, he's lying!"

"Did you kiss him?" Suzanne asked, her voice shaking. "Did you?" She looked again at the rumpled bed.

"He kissed me!"

"What kind of friend are you?" Suzanne cried. "You and I both know that you've been after Gregory since Tristan died."

"But he's been after me since—" Ivy saw Gregory glance at her out of the corner of his eye, and she broke off her sentence.

She knew she had lost the battle.

Suzanne was trembling so, she could hardly get the words out. "Leave," she said in a low, husky voice. "Get out of here, Ivy. Don't ever come back."

"I'll clean up—"

"Leave! Just leave!" Suzanne shouted.

There was nothing she could do. Ivy left her friend crying and clinging to Gregory.

11

Ivy didn't think about how she was getting home. She ducked into a bathroom farther down the hall and washed her mouth out with toothpaste. After buttoning and tucking in the blouse, she raced downstairs, snatched up her purse, and hurried out of the house.

She struggled to hold back the tears. She didn't want Gregory to hear stories later on about how upset she was. Philip's words came back to her once more. "He can smell it if you're afraid."

Now Ivy was terrified—for both herself and her friends. At any point they could stumble upon one of Gregory's secrets. And his ego was big enough, he was crazy enough to assume that he could get away with silencing not just her, but Suzanne, Will, and Beth, too.

Ivy walked briskly along the side of Lantern Road. The houses in Suzanne's neighborhood were far apart, and there were no sidewalks. It was another dark mile to the intersection and two more miles into the town itself. The only light was a soft yellow moon.

"Angels, stay with me," Ivy prayed.

She had walked about a third of a mile when the headlights of a car bore down on her. She stepped quickly off the road and ducked into some bushes. The car drove ten feet more, then screeched to a halt. Ivy scrambled to get deeper into the brush. The driver suddenly extinguished his bright lights, and she could see the shape of the car in the moonlight: a Honda. Will's car.

He climbed out and looked around. "Ivy?"

She wanted to rush out of the bushes and into his arms, but she held back.

"Ivy, if you're here, tell me. Tell me you're okay."

Her mind raced, trying to think what she could tell him without spilling the whole and dangerous truth.

"Answer me. Are you okay? Lacey said you were in trouble. Tell me if there is some way I can help."

Even in the pale light, the look of worry on his face was visible. She longed to reach out to him and tell him everything. She wanted to run to him and feel his arms wrap around her, keeping her safe for a moment. But for his sake she couldn't—she knew that. Her eyes burned. She blinked several times to clear them, then emerged onto the road.

"Ivy." He breathed her name.

"I—I was going home," she said.

His glance flicked to the bushes behind her. "Taking a shortcut?"

"Maybe you could give me a ride," she said softly.

He studied her face a moment, then silently opened the door for her. When he had locked and closed it again, Ivy leaned against the door, feeling safe. She would be safe till she got to the house on the ridge.

Will got in on the driver's side. "Do you really want to go home?" he asked.

In the end, she'd have to. She nodded, but he didn't start the car.

"Ivy, who are you afraid of?"

She shrugged and looked down at her hands. "I don't know."

Will reached over and laid his hand on top of hers. She turned it over and examined the small flecks of oil paint that the turpentine rag had missed. Ivy could picture Will's hands with her eyes closed. The way his fingers felt now entwined with hers made her feel strong.

"I want to help you," he said, "but I can't if I don't know what's going on."

Ivy turned her face away from him.

"You have to tell me what's going on," he insisted.

"I can't, Will."

"What happened that night at the train station?" he asked.

She didn't answer him.

"You must remember something now. You must have some idea about what you saw. Was someone else there? What made you try to cross the tracks?"

She shook her head and said nothing.

"All right," he said in a resigned voice. "Then I've got just one more question for you. Are you in love with Gregory?"

Ivy was caught off guard, and her head spun toward him. Will looked into her eyes. He studied her whole face. "That's what I needed to know," he said quietly.

What had she given away? Ivy wondered. What had her eyes revealed? That she hated Gregory? Or that she was falling in love with Will?

She let go of his hand. "Please take me home," she said, and he did.

"And now," said a voice quivering with emotion, "we return to today's program . . . *For Love of Ivy*." A soap opera tune was hummed loudly—and pretty badly, Tristan thought.

Will heard it, too. He glanced around the school darkroom, where he had been working alone, and saw Lacey's purple shimmer. "You again," he muttered.

As always, Tristan found it remarkably easy to match thoughts with Will. He slipped quickly inside him, so he could communicate with both Will and Lacey.

Will blinked. "Tristan?" he said aloud.

"Yeah," he replied. The soap opera music continued in the background. "You're off key, Lacey," Tristan told her.

The humming stopped, and the purple shimmer moved closer to him and Will.

Will quickly put a roll of film behind him. "Could you step back a little, Lacey? You might expose my film."

"Well, ex*cuse* me!" she replied. "I guess you two heroes don't need me around. I'll be on my way." She paused to give them time to protest. When neither of them did, she added, "But before I go, let me ask you lover boys a few questions. Who got Rip van Winkle here out of the darkness before the next hundred years had passed? Who directed him to this darkroom?"

"I've been calling for you, Tristan," Will explained. "I need your help."

"Who played guardian angel at Suzanne's party?" Lacey continued. "Who told you when Ivy was in big trouble?"

"Ivy was in trouble? What happened?" Tristan asked.

"Who, tell me, *who's* playing secretary to this pitiful Ivy fan club?"

"Tell me what happened," Tristan demanded. "Is Ivy okay?"

"Yes and no," Will replied, then told Tristan about the incident at the party, including Gregory's account of it. "I don't know what really happened," he said. "I caught up with Ivy afterward on the road. She was upset and wouldn't tell me anything. On Sunday she worked, then went straight to Beth's. At school today she'd talk only to Beth but wouldn't tell even her what really happened."

"Lacey, did you see anything?" Tristan asked.

"Sorry, I was, uh, socializing at the time."

"What do you think she was doing?" Tristan asked.

"Throwing the shoes of ungrateful movie fans into the pond," Will told him.

"I'm talking about Ivy!" Tristan snapped, but he was more upset with himself than Will. Twice now Will had been there for Ivy when Tristan had not.

"I've been calling you—" Will began.

"And calling and calling," Lacey said. "I told him you were in the darkness. I knew love was blind, but I guess it's deaf too. I guess—"

"You've got to tell me some things, Tristan," Will interrupted her. "You've got to tell me now. How can I help Ivy if I don't know what's going on?"

"But you know enough," Tristan challenged him. "More than you've admitted to Ivy." He began to probe Will's mind, but was swiftly pushed aside. "I know you looked in the envelope, Will," Tristan said. "I was watching when you pulled out the key."

Will didn't seem surprised or apologetic. He slipped the film into a canister. "What does the key go to?" he asked.

"I thought you might have figured it out," Tristan baited him.

"No."

Tristan tried again to probe Will's thoughts, completely silencing his own, moving slowly and carefully. He got slammed like a hockey player against the wall of Will's mind.

"Okay, okay, you two, what's going on?" Lacey

asked. "I can see your face, Will. You've got the same pigheaded expression that Tristan gets."

"He's blocking me out," Tristan charged.

"Like you haven't done the same thing to me," Will replied heatedly. "First you send me racing up the ridge to save Ivy's life. I let you take over. I go along with you and do just what you say, and I find Ivy with a bag over her head. Gregory's there with a strange excuse, but you won't tell me a thing about what's going on."

Will set down the canister and walked up and down the narrow room, picking up and putting down filters, markers, boxes of paper. "You get me to speak for you. You get me to dance with her and warn her and tell her you love her." Will's voice trembled a little. "But you don't tell me anything to explain why this is happening."

Ivy won't let me, Tristan thought, but he knew that wasn't the only reason. He resented the fact that he needed Will, and he didn't like the way Will was calling some of the shots now.

"I don't like this mind-control stuff," Will went on angrily. "I don't like your trying to read my mind. If there's something you want to know, ask it."

"What I want to know," Tristan said, "is how I'm supposed to trust you. You're Gregory's friend—"

"Oh, grow up, you two!" Lacey interrupted. "I don't like mind control. How can I trust you?" she mimicked. "*Puh-lease* don't bore me with the rest of your excuses. You're both in love with Ivy, and you're jealous of each other, and that's why you're keeping your little secrets and squabbling like two kindergarten kids."

"*Are* you in love with her, Will?" Tristan asked quickly.

He felt Will thinking, he felt Will dodging him.

Will picked up the film canister again and shifted it from hand to hand. "I'm trying to do what's best for her," he said at last.

"You didn't answer my question."

"I don't see why it matters," Will argued. "You were there when I danced with her. You heard what Ivy said. We both know she'll never love anyone the way she loves you."

"We both know you hope it's not true," Tristan replied.

Will slammed the canister down on the table. "I've got work to do."

"So do I," Tristan said, and slipped out of Will before he could be thrown out.

He knew that Ivy would love someone else someday and that that person might be Will. Well, if he had to leave her in Will's hands, he was going to check him out thoroughly first.

As Tristan left the darkroom he heard Lacey's soap opera voice. "And so our two heroes part," she said, "blinded by love, neither of them listening to the wise and beautiful Lacey"—she hummed a little—"who, by the way, is getting a broken heart of her own. But who cares about Lacey?" she asked sadly. "Who cares about Lacey?"

12

Ivy sat at the kitchen table glancing over legal forms that she had just pulled out of a manila envelope—Philip's adoption papers. Across from her, her brother and his best friend Sammy dug spoons into a peanut butter jar.

Sammy was a short, funny-looking kid whose hair stood straight up from his head like bristly red grass. Ivy saw him eyeing her. He nudged Philip. "Ask her. Ask her."

"Ask me what?"

"Sammy wants to meet Tristan," Philip said. "But I can't get him to come. Do you know where he is?"

Ivy instinctively glanced over her shoulder, but Philip assured her, "It's okay. Mom's upstairs, and Gregory likes to hear about angels now."

"He does?" Ivy asked with surprise.

Philip nodded.

"I really want to see an angel," Sammy said, pulling a little camera out of his grubby school pack.

Ivy smiled. "I think Tristan's resting now," she said, then she turned to Philip. "What kind of angel things have you and Gregory been talking about?"

"He asked me about Tristan."

"What exactly did he want to know?" Ivy asked.

She had suspected that the train incident haunted Gregory. After all, there was no way Philip could have gotten to the station that quickly without help from someone. Did Gregory guess that he was up against more than herself, more than just a person?

"He asked me what Tristan looked like," Philip told her. "And how I know when he's there."

"And how to get him to come," Sammy said. "Remember, he asked that."

"He wanted to know if you ever talked to Tristan," Philip added.

Ivy tapped the manila envelope against the table. "When did you talk about all this?"

"Last night," her brother replied, "when we were playing in the tree house."

Ivy frowned. She didn't like the idea of Gregory's playing with Philip up in the tree house, where one accident had already occurred during the summer.

She glanced down at the adoption forms. Andrew hadn't told Gregory that he was about to make Philip his legal son. Ivy wondered if Andrew had the same kind of fears that she did.

"When will Tristan be finished with his nap?" Sammy asked.

"I don't really know," Ivy replied.

"I have a flashlight, in case I see him at night," he told her.

"Good idea," Ivy said with a smile. She watched as the two boys licked the last bit of peanut butter off their spoons and ran outside.

Since Saturday night, she too had been trying to reach Tristan. Rumors about the party were flying at school. Gregory and she had managed to avoid each other in the halls. So had she and Suzanne, but while Gregory slipped past Ivy, Suzanne dramatically played out each snub. Her anger at Ivy was obvious to everyone.

Ivy was relieved when Beth had told her that Gregory and Suzanne were going to the football game that afternoon. Having slept little in the past two nights, she could finally rest, knowing that Gregory wouldn't walk in on her. Even though she locked her bedroom door now, she never really felt safe.

Ivy slipped the envelope and forms in her stack of schoolbooks and was about to head upstairs when she heard a car pull up behind the house. It sounded like Gregory's BMW. Her first instinct was to rush up to her room, but she didn't want Gregory to think she was afraid of him. Sitting back down, she opened the newspaper and hunched over the table, pretending to read. The kitchen door was pushed open, and instantly Ivy smelled the perfume. "Suzanne."

Suzanne responded with a sullen look.

"Hi," Gregory said. His tone of voice was neither warm nor cold, and his face was expressionless—though ready to flash into a smile if anyone else happened to walk into the kitchen. Suzanne continued to look at Ivy with pouting lips.

"This is a surprise," Ivy said. "Beth said you were going to the football game."

"Suzanne was bored, and I had to pick up something," Gregory told her. He turned his back to Ivy, reached into the cupboard, and pulled out a tall copper cup. "Would you get her a drink?" he asked, handing Ivy the cup.

"Sure." Gregory exited the kitchen quickly.

Ivy checked the refrigerator for sodas. "Sorry, no cold ones," she told Suzanne.

Suzanne remained silent.

Except you, Ivy said to herself, then reached under the counter for a bottle. She wondered why Gregory would leave them alone to talk. Perhaps he was standing outside the kitchen door, waiting to hear what she would say. Maybe this was a test to see if she'd tell Suzanne what she knew about him.

"How are you doing?" Ivy asked.

"Fine."

A one-word answer, but it was a start. Ivy dropped some ice cubes into the soda and handed it to Suzanne. "At school a lot of kids were talking about your party. Everyone had a good time."

"Downstairs and upstairs," Suzanne replied.

Ivy remained silent.

"How bad was your hangover?" Suzanne asked.

"I didn't have one," Ivy told her.

"Oh, that's right, you got rid of all the booze in you."

Ivy bit her lip.

"I couldn't sleep in my room Saturday night," Suzanne said, and walked around the kitchen, swirling the drink in her cup.

"I'm sorry about that, Suzanne. I really am. But the truth is, I didn't have anything to drink," Ivy said firmly.

"I want to believe you." Suzanne's lip trembled. "I want you and Gregory to tell me I dreamed it all."

"You know he won't. And I won't, either."

Suzanne nodded and dropped her chin. "I know everybody cries when they break up with a guy. But I never thought I'd get out the tissues because I was splitting up with you."

"You've known me longer than any of your guys," Ivy replied quickly. "You trusted me for ten years. Then one guy says something, and you don't."

"I saw you with my own eyes!"

"What did you see?" Ivy almost shouted. "You saw what he wanted you to see, what he told you to see. How can I convince you—"

"You can stop fooling around with my boyfriend, that's how! You can keep your hot little hands where they belong!" Suzanne took a large gulp of her drink. "You're making a fool of yourself, Ivy, and you're doing it at my expense."

"Suzanne, why can't you admit that it's at least possible that Gregory was coming on to me?"

"*Liar*," Suzanne said. "I'll never trust you again." She took another angry gulp of soda, leaving a print of her lipstick on the shiny metal. "I warned you, Ivy. But you didn't listen to me. You didn't care enough to."

"I care about you more than you realize," Ivy said, taking a step toward Suzanne.

Suzanne turned on her heel. "Tell Gregory I'm on the patio," she said as she walked out the kitchen door.

Ivy let her friend go. It's useless, she thought. He's poisoned Suzanne's mind. Fighting back the tears, Ivy rushed out of the kitchen toward the stairs. She ran headlong into Gregory and pushed past him. She didn't bother telling him where Suzanne had gone. She was sure he had been listening to every word.

Ivy didn't pause to catch her breath until she reached her music room. She slammed the door closed behind her and leaned against it. Keep cool, keep cool, she said to herself.

But she couldn't stop shaking. She had lost all hope that she could win against Gregory. She needed help, needed someone to assure her that things would get better. She remembered the day Will had driven her back to the train station, how he had believed in her and given her the confidence to believe in herself.

"I'll find Will," she said aloud, then turned toward the door and was surprised to see the shimmering gold light. "Tristan!"

His gold light surrounded her. "Yes, *Tristan*," he said, within her now.

"Are you all right? Where have you been?" Ivy asked silently. "You were gone so long this time. A lot has happened since you fell into the darkness."

"I know," Tristan replied. "Will and Lacey filled me in."

"Did they tell you about Suzanne? She thinks— she believes whatever Gregory says, and she hates me now, she—" The flood of tears was uncontrollable.

"Shhh. Ivy, shhh. I know about Suzanne," Tristan told her. "And I'm sorry, but you have to forget about her right now. There are a lot more import—"

"Forget about her?" The tears became furious ones, and Ivy spoke out loud. "He wants to hurt me any and every way he can!"

"Ivy, speak silently," Tristan reminded her quickly. "I know this is hard for you—"

"You don't know! You don't understand how I feel," Ivy said, sitting down at the piano. She ran her finger sharply up the keyboard.

"Listen to me, Ivy. I found out something you have to know."

"I can't keep losing people," she said.

"There's something I want to tell you about," Tristan persisted.

"First I lost you, now Suzanne, and—"

"Will," he said.

"Will?" The tone of Tristan's voice, low and firm, alarmed her. "What about Will?" she asked, crossing her arms.

"You can't trust him."

"But I do trust him," Ivy replied, determined not to be persuaded otherwise.

"I just came from searching his house," Tristan told her.

"Searching?"

"And I found some pretty interesting things there," he added.

"Like what?" she demanded.

"Books about angels. A tracing of Caroline's key."

"Well, what do you expect?" Ivy asked. "Of course he's read about angels. He's trying to understand exactly what you are and why you've come back. And we already knew he was curious enough to look in the envelope that contained the key. I would have done the same thing if I were him," she added defensively.

"There was also a copy of Beth's story," Tristan said. "The one about the woman who committed suicide, the one she recited for your drama club assignment the month before Caroline died. Do you remember it?"

Ivy nodded slowly. "The woman tore up photographs of her lover and his new sweetheart, leaving them like a suicide note when she shot herself."

"Just as Caroline supposedly tore up photos of Andrew and your mother," Tristan said.

Once before Ivy had thought about the similarity

between Beth's story and the setup the police had found at Caroline's house. She had assumed it was another example of the uncanny way Beth anticipated events, but now she realized that Gregory could have borrowed the idea from Beth.

"And there's a clipping of the story about the girl in Ridgefield," Tristan went on. "The one who was attacked right after you were, in the exact same way. It worked, didn't it? The style of attack convinced everyone that it was part of a series of crimes by someone who didn't know you."

Ivy dropped her head in her hands, thinking about the girl.

"So what are you saying?" she asked at last. "That Will has figured out a lot more than we thought? I'm glad. I wanted to protect him, but now there's no reason to hold anything back."

"But there is a reason," Tristan replied quickly. "Will has something else. The jacket and cap."

Ivy sat up straight. How had he gotten the clothes? Did he know they were important evidence? Why hadn't he told her?

"Oh, he knows they're important," Tristan answered her thoughts. "They were wrapped carefully in plastic bags and hidden with everything else."

"But I never told him what I saw. I never told him what tempted me to cross the tracks, and that story wasn't released to the papers."

"So either he was in on it—"

"No!" said Ivy.

"—or he's somehow figured it out. Maybe Eric told him something. In any case, he knows a lot more than he's telling either of us."

Ivy remembered the day at the station when they had caught Eric searching the drainage ditch by the side of the road. Will must have already found the cap and jacket. He was faking it in front of Eric—and her.

She stood up abruptly, pushing back the piano bench.

"Ivy?"

She mentally pushed Tristan away and walked over to the window. Dropping down on her knees, Ivy rested her arms and chin on the windowsill.

"Ivy, talk to me. Don't push me away."

"He's just trying to help us," Ivy said. "I'm sure it's nothing more than that."

"How can he be helping when he's hiding things from us?"

"Because he thinks that's what's best," she replied, though she knew it didn't make sense. "I know him. I trust him."

"Suzanne trusts Gregory," Tristan pointed out.

"It's not the same!" Ivy cried, thrusting Tristan out of her mind altogether. "It's not the same!"

She had cried out loud, and for a moment she thought she heard her own voice reverberating in the room. Then she realized the shouting came from below. Suzanne was calling out. Ivy heard Gregory's voice drowning out Suzanne's. She rushed down to her bedroom and raced across the second-floor hall to the back set of steps. Suzanne was hurrying up the narrow stair, her long black hair fanning out behind her, her face pale and glistening with perspiration. She clutched the copper cup in which Ivy had fixed her soda.

Gregory trailed her. "Suzanne," he said, "give Ivy a chance to explain."

Suzanne threw back her head and laughed wildly, so wildly she almost fell backward down the stair. Then she looked at Ivy, and Ivy knew something was terribly wrong.

"I can't wait," Suzanne said. "I can't wait to see how she explains this one."

Suzanne shoved the soda toward Ivy, forcing her to take the cup in her hands. Then she uncurled her left fist. In the damp palm of her friend's hand, Ivy saw a round orange pill. Ivy glanced quickly at Gregory, then back at the tablet.

"What is it?" Suzanne asked. "Tell me, what did I find in my drink?"

"It looks like a vitamin," Ivy said cautiously.

"A vitamin!" Suzanne shrieked with laughter, but Ivy saw the tears in her friend's eyes. "That's good," Suzanne sputtered. "A vitamin. What were you going to do, Ivy? Send me on a nice trip like Eric's? You're crazy. You're a screwed-up, crazy, jealous witch." She dropped the orange tablet in the soda. "Here, let's put the vitamin back. Now you drink it, drink all of it."

Ivy stared down at the copper-colored cup. She knew that Gregory had set her up, and she figured it was harmless, but she couldn't take the chance.

"Swallow it," Suzanne said, tears running down her face. "Swallow the vitamin."

Ivy put her hand over the top of the cup and shook her head. She saw Suzanne's mouth jerk.

Suzanne turned, ducked under Gregory's arms, and ran down to the first floor. Gregory followed her. Ivy sank down on the steps and dropped her head to her knees. She didn't try to hide the tears, though she knew that Gregory paused to look over his shoulder, enjoying the view.

13

Tristan thought that warning Ivy about Will would have made him feel good. After all, his suspicions were right. Will was not admitting to them what he knew, and he wasn't telling them how he knew it. Now Ivy could trust only Tristan. He should have felt smart and victorious—at least satisfied. He didn't. No matter how much they needed and loved each other, he and Ivy stood on either side of an uncrossable river.

Monday evening the world seemed grayer, chillier to him. He stood outside of Caroline's dark house and felt the autumn coming on like a creature who has no home. When Tristan slipped through the walls, he felt like an intruder, a ghost who haunted, not an angel who helped those he loved. He longed to be with Ivy, but he didn't dare go to her now. He knew the information about Will had hurt and angered her. Now that he had told her, what could Tristan say to make things better?

"Tristan?"

He looked around, surprised.

"Tristan?"

He wanted so much to hear Ivy's voice that he thought he did.

"Are you in there?" she called. "Let me in."

Tristan hurried to the door, focusing quickly in order to materialize his fingers. They kept slipping on the latch as he struggled to undo it. He wondered if it looked strange to Ivy when the door of the darkened house swung slowly in on its hinges.

She stepped inside and stopped just within the moonlit rectangle made by the gaping door. In the silver light her hair shimmered, and her skin looked as pale as an apparition's. For a moment Tristan believed something terrible and wonderful had happened, and she had come to him as a spirit like himself. But then he saw how she turned toward him, her eyes full of love but unfocused, the way eyes see a glow, but not the features of a face.

"I love you." They shared that thought, and he moved easily inside her mind.

"I'm sorry, Tristan," she said softly. "I'm sorry I pushed you out like that."

He was so glad to be with her, so glad she had come to him, he couldn't speak for a moment. "I know I hurt you when I told you about Will," he said at last.

She gave a little shrug and closed the door behind them. "You had to tell me the truth."

Tristan knew from the small shrug that the news still upset her. I should make her talk about it, he thought. I should remind her that she'll fall in love again, there will be someone else she'll love one day—

"I love you, Tristan," Ivy said. "Please, no matter what happens, promise you won't forget that."

Another time. They could talk about the future another time.

"Are you listening?" Ivy asked. "I know you're there. You're cloaking, Tristan. Are you angry?"

"I'm wondering," he said. "How did you know to come here?"

He felt the smile on her lips. "I'm not sure," she said. "I guess I just needed to see you so badly, and after this afternoon, I didn't think you'd come when I called. I figured it was up to me to find you. I got in the car and drove, and here's where I ended up."

He laughed. "Here's where you ended up. After all this is over, you and Beth are going to have to open a shop—Palms, Tea Leaves, and Telepathy."

"You could join us for séances," Ivy suggested. Her smile warmed him through.

"Lyons, Van Dyke, and Spirit. Sounds good," he said, but he knew that when his mission was over he wouldn't come back. None of the angels Lacey had known ever returned.

Ivy was still smiling as she walked around Caroline's kitchen. He saw through her eyes as they slowly adjusted to the dark. "It looks as if you've been searching the house," she said, observing the open kitchen drawers and cabinet doors that hung ajar.

"Lacey and I searched here back in August, long before you got the key, but we didn't leave the place like this," he replied. "Someone else has been here since."

He heard the thought, though she tried hard to repress it. Will.

"It could have been a lot of people," Tristan said quickly. "Gregory or Eric. Or Will," he added as softly as possible. "Or even that guy who visits Caroline's grave and leaves her red roses."

"I saw a long-stemmed rose there."

"Did you see him?" Tristan asked as Ivy peeked inside the open cupboards. Most of them were empty, but she found a flashlight in a shallow drawer.

"No. What's he look like?"

"Tall, slim, dark-haired," Tristan replied. "His name is Tom Stetson, and he works at Andrew's college. Lacey followed him around at your Labor Day party. Ever hear anyone talk about him?"

Ivy shook her head, then said suddenly, "If I shake my head, or make a face, I guess you don't know it when you're inside me."

"I know it. I feel it. I love it when you smile."

The smile grew so that it seemed to wrap itself around him.

"So what do you think?" Ivy asked. "Was Tom Stetson Caroline's new love? Was he involved somehow?"

"I don't know," Tristan said, "but both he and

Gregory must have a key to this house. I think Tom's the one who's been boxing things up."

"And searching through cupboards and drawers at the same time," Ivy said.

"Maybe."

She reached for the string around her neck and pulled out the key that was dangling beneath her shirt. Under the beam of the flashlight, its silver shaft and two jagged teeth gleamed.

"Well, I'm the one who's got the key," she said. "Now if we can just find the lock . . ."

They began to search together. In the living room they discovered a desk with a locked drawer which had been forced open. Close by, on the mantel, was a box with a brass lock whose hinges had been broken. It now lay empty. Ivy tested the key in both locks and found that it had not been made for either.

In the bedroom Tristan called Ivy's attention to a rectangular design pressed into a bureau cloth, as if a heavy box had sat there for a long time but was gone now. Caroline's closet was still full of shoes and purses, which looked as if they had been searched. Ivy pulled them out and felt behind them. They moved on to other rooms. An hour and a half later, their search had turned up nothing.

"There's a lot of junk here, but we're not getting anywhere," Tristan said, frustrated.

Ivy sank down in the corner of the hallway. He noticed that she avoided sitting in any of Caroline's chairs.

"The problem is, we don't know what's been carried out of here already or where it's been carried to," Ivy observed. "If only we had some clue about what we were looking for."

"How about Beth?" Tristan asked suddenly. "What if we got her to help? She has a sixth sense. Maybe if you show her the key, let her hold it and meditate on it, she'll be able to tell us where to look—at least give us a hint."

"Good idea." Ivy glanced at her watch. "Can you come with me?"

Tristan knew that he shouldn't. He was tired and needed to pace himself if he wanted to keep from falling into the darkness. But he couldn't give her up. Something told him there was not much time left for him to spend with Ivy.

"I'll come, but I'd better just observe," he said. He was quiet most of the way to Beth's house.

Mr. Van Dyke must have been getting used to Ivy's calling at unexpected times. Standing in the doorway, he glanced at her over his half glasses and law brief, hollered "Beth!" and left Ivy to find her way upstairs.

Tristan was startled by the sight of Beth and her room, but Ivy told him silently, "She's been writing."

Beth blinked at Ivy as if she were worlds away. A binder clip held her hair in a lopsided ponytail. An old pair of glasses sat partway down her nose; they also were lopsided, since they were missing an arm. She wore baggy gym shorts and scuzzy-looking slippers with animal heads on them and popcorn embedded in their fur.

Ivy reached toward Beth and pulled a yellow Post-it off her T-shirt. "'Lovely, lingering, delicate, devious, delicious,'" she read, then said, "I'm really sorry about barging in like this."

"That's okay," Beth replied cheerfully, and reached for the Post-it. "I was looking for this—thanks."

"It's just that we need your help."

"We? Oh." Beth closed the bedroom door quickly and cleared a spot on the bed, dumping folders and notebooks on the floor. She studied Ivy's face, then smiled. "Hello, Mr. Glow," she said to Tristan.

"Beth, do you remember the envelope Eric's sister gave me?"
Ivy asked.

Tristan saw the sudden brightness in Beth's eyes. She had watched Ivy open the envelope at the cemetery and must have been dying with curiosity.

"This is what was in it." Ivy pulled out the key and placed it in Beth's hand.

"It looks as if it goes to a box," Beth said, "or a drawer. It could be an old door key, but I don't think so—it doesn't look long enough."

"The envelope it came in had Caroline's name and address on it," Ivy said. "We've been searching her house but can't find what it goes to. Can you work on it? You know, keep it for a while and think about it and see if anything comes to you?"

Tristan saw Beth draw back. "Oh, Ivy, I—"

"Please."

"She's afraid," Tristan said softly to Ivy. "You have

to help her. Her own predictions have frightened her."

"I'm not asking you to predict anything," Ivy said quickly. "Just hold it and think about it and see what comes to you. No matter how strange or ordinary it seems, it may be a clue to tell us where to look."

Beth looked down at the key. "I wish you hadn't asked me, Ivy. When I do something like this, it stirs up all kinds of other things in my mind, things I don't understand, things that frighten me sometimes." She turned and looked longingly at the computer screen on her desk, where the cursor blinked, waiting for her to return to her story. "I wish you hadn't asked me."

"Okay, I understand," Ivy said, picking up the key.

Beth's hand closed around Ivy's. Tristan could feel how cold and clammy it was. "Leave it with me till tomorrow," she said. "I'll give it back to you at school. Maybe something will come to me."

Ivy threw her arms around her friend. "Thank you. Thank you. I wouldn't have asked you if it weren't important."

A few minutes later Ivy headed home. "You're still with me," she said as she turned up the long driveway.

The happiness in her voice warmed Tristan, but he could not throw off his weariness and a growing sense of dread that the darkness would soon overtake him. What if he was in the darkness when Ivy needed him most?

"I'll stay with you until you get to your room," he said. "Then I'll return to Beth's."

As they passed a bush Ivy suddenly bent down. "Ella? Ella, come out and say hello. Your buddy is with me."

The cat's green eyes glinted at them, but she didn't budge.

"Ella, come on, what's wrong?"

Ella mewed, and Ivy reached into the bushes to pull her out. She lifted up the cat, rubbing her in her favorite spot around her ears. The cat didn't purr.

"What's wrong with you?" Ivy said, then gasped. Tristan felt the shudder run through her as if it rippled through his own body. Ivy turned the cat over gently. Along her right flank was a stripe where fur had been roughly stripped away. Her pink skin was scraped bloody and raw.

"Ella, how did this—" But Ivy didn't finish the question. She realized the answer the same moment Tristan did. "Gregory," she said.

14

All night Ivy had dreams about Ella, long, winding dreams in which Gregory chased the cat and Ivy chased Gregory. Then just as she got close, he turned on her. Ivy's sleep did not grow peaceful until after the sky was light. Now, with eyes closed against the brightness, she counted the muted gongs from the clock in the dining room. They sounded a million miles away—five million, six million, seven million, eight million—

"Eight!" She sat up quickly in bed.

Ella, who had been snuggled close, pressed her body hard against Ivy's, burying her face in Ivy's side. As gently as possible, Ivy lifted the cat onto her lap. When she saw the wound again, tears came to her eyes. "Okay, girl, let's clean you up."

She carefully lifted Ella off the bed and carried her toward the bathroom.

"Ivy, Ivy, aren't you ready yet?" her mother called from downstairs.

Ivy turned and walked out to the hall, staying close enough to the wall to remain hidden from Maggie. "Almost," she called down.

"Everyone else is gone," Maggie shouted back at her. "I'm leaving now, too."

"See you," Ivy said with relief.

She heard the click-click of her mother's heels on the hardwood floors and the sound of the back door closing. Then she lifted Ella up to her face to look at the wound again. The cut was straight, as if made by a sharp razor.

The previous night Tristan had had to use all of his powers of persuasion to restrain her from charging into Gregory's room. This morning she knew Tristan had been right to hold her back. She'd confront Gregory, but when she was cool and calm. Gregory wanted to see her upset, and her anger would just encourage him.

"Okay, baby, everything's going to be all right," Ivy soothed Ella as she reentered her room.

The morning sun was high enough now to flood the room and stream across the top of her bureau, brightening every speck of dust and picking up flecks of gold paint in the frame around Tristan's picture. Ivy gazed at the picture for a moment, then pulled back. In front of it were shavings of black hair—Ella's fur. Ivy held Ella against her with one arm and reached out to touch the soft fur. Then she picked up a lock of curling gold hair.

Her hair! Someone had cut a piece of her own hair.

Gregory, of course. Ivy sank down into a chair next to the bureau and rocked back and forth, hugging Ella. When had he done it? How?

Every night since the day Tristan had told her what he knew about Gregory, Ivy had locked the bedroom door that led to the hall. There was another entrance, however, through the bathroom that connected her room and Philip's. Ivy had rigged the latch on that door so that Philip could push it open in an emergency, but not without a lot of effort and noise. Somehow Gregory had worked it silently. Her skin prickled all over, thinking of him holding a pair of scissors, bending over her while she was asleep.

Ivy took a deep breath and stood up again. She cleaned up Ella, then wiped off the top of the bureau, her hands still trembling. Then on a sudden impulse she rushed into Gregory's room, wanting to see for herself the scissors, the razor, the proof of what he had done.

She started picking up and throwing papers and clothes and magazines. From between the pages of *Rolling Stone* a piece of art paper slipped out. It was folded in half and had dark printing inside. When Ivy opened it, her heart stopped. She recognized the handwriting instantly: the strong, slanting style was identical to that of the captions on Will's cartoons.

She read through the note quickly, then read it again very slowly, word by word, like a first grader surprised by each set of printed letters and what they meant. As she read Will's note she kept telling herself that these weren't his words—they couldn't be. But he had signed it.

"Gregory," he had written, "I want more. If you're serious about it, you'll bring twice the amount. I'm taking a chance, I'm an accomplice now—you've got to make it worth it. Bring twice the money if you want the cap and jacket."

Ivy closed her eyes and leaned against Gregory's desk. She felt as if her heart were being squeezed, transformed into a small stone. When all was done, there would be nothing soft left inside her, nothing left that could bleed . . . or cry.

She opened her eyes again. Tristan had been right all along about Gregory and Will. But Tristan hadn't guessed how Will would betray her—how he'd cover for Gregory and leave her vulnerable if paid the right price.

Ivy felt beaten, not by Gregory's hatred and dark threats, but by the pale heartlessness of Will. What was the point of trying? she thought. There was too much going against her. She slipped the letter back in the magazine. Then she saw a tattered book about Babe Ruth, one of Philip's paperbacks, on top of Gregory's pile.

She had to keep going. Philip was in this with her.

Opening the magazine again, she snatched up the letter, then hurried back across the hall to dress for school. Before leaving the house that morning, Ivy brought Ella's water bowl and dry food up to her room. She left Ella there, locking both the bathroom and hall doors.

Ivy had missed homeroom. When she entered English class with a late slip, Beth lifted her head. She looked tired and worried. Ivy winked, and Beth smiled a little.

After class they walked together, trying to get away from the crowd of kids surging through the hall. Nothing could be heard over the talk and banging locker doors unless it was shouted. Ivy linked arms with her friend and opened the palm of her hand. Immediately Beth slipped the key into it.

When they finally reached an empty room at the end of the corridor, Beth said, "Ivy, we have to talk. I had a dream last night. I don't know what it means, but I think—"

The school bell rang.

"Oh, no, I've got a test next period."

"Lunchtime," Ivy said. "Try for the table back in the corner," she added as they parted.

Two hours later Ivy got lucky. Ms. Bryce, the school counselor, let her out early for lunch, saying how pleased she was by Ivy's progress, her fresh hope and positive attitude toward life. I guess drama club pays off, Ivy thought as she staked out the small table in the corner of the cafeteria. Beth joined her a few minutes later.

"Will's in line. Should I wave him over here?" Beth asked.

Ivy chewed her sandwich quickly and swallowed hard. Will was the last person in the world she wanted to see. But Beth still trusted him. She was already signaling to him.

"Did you mention anything to Will about the key or our search?" Ivy asked.

"No."

"Good," Ivy said. "Don't. I don't want him to know about it—not yet," she added, softening her tone when she saw the surprised look on Beth's face.

"But Will might have some good ideas," Beth said, opening her lunch bag, pulling out her usual first course—dessert. "I'm sure he'd want to help you search."

No doubt, thought Ivy. Who knows what he'd find that might be worth some money.

"You know how he feels about you," Beth added.

Ivy couldn't squelch her sarcasm. "Oh, yeah, I know, all right."

Beth blinked at her. "Ivy, he'd do anything for you."

And make some bucks while doing it, Ivy thought, but this time she spoke more carefully. "Maybe you're right, Beth, but still, don't tell him, okay?"

Beth's eyebrows drew together. She wouldn't argue further, but she clearly thought Ivy was making a mistake.

"Tell me what you dreamed last night," Ivy said.

Her friend shook her head slowly. "It was weird, Ivy, so simple but so weird. I dreamed the same thing over and over. I don't know if it had anything to do with the key, but it was about you."

"Tell me," Ivy said, leaning close to her while keeping one eye on Will's progress in the cafeteria line.

"There were these big wheels," Beth recalled, "two, three, I don't know how many. Big wheels with rough edges, notches in them, like tractor wheels or snow tires or something. They were all turning one way. Then you came. There was nothing else in the dream but you and the wheels. You put out your hand and stopped them. Then you pushed, and the wheels all started spinning the opposite way."

She fell silent. Her eyes had a faraway look, as if she were seeing the dream again.

"And?"

"That's it," Beth said. "That's all I dreamed, over and over."

Ivy sat back in her chair, puzzled. "Do you have any idea what it means?" she asked.

"I was going to ask you the same thing," Beth replied. "Ivy, here comes Will. Why don't we tell him and—"

"No," she said quickly.

Beth bit her lip. Ivy looked down at the soggy layers of her sandwich.

"Hi!" said Will, scraping back a chair and setting down his tray. "What's up?"

"Nothing much," Ivy said, avoiding his eyes.

"Beth?"

"Nothing much," she echoed lamely.

Will was silent for a moment. "How come you were late this morning?" he asked Ivy.

She glanced up sharply. "How do you know I was late?"

"Because I was, too." Will tilted his head a little, as if he was trying to read her.

169

Ivy looked away.

"I came in just after you," he said, then reached for her hand, touching her lightly, trying to get her to look at him again. She would not.

"What's wrong?"

She hated the innocent and concerned tone of his voice.

"Beth? Tell me what it is."

Ivy peeked up at her friend. Beth shrugged, and Will glanced back and forth between them. His face was calm and thoughtful, like that of a teacher patiently searching for an answer, but his hands gave him away, gripping the edge of his tray.

Now he's worried, Ivy thought, really worried, but not about me. He thinks we both know the truth about him.

Will sucked in his breath, then said quietly, "Surprise. Here comes Gregory."

Ivy looked up, hoping to see Suzanne with him. If Suzanne put in her usual effort at snubbing her, Ivy would have an excuse to walk out. But Gregory came alone, striding confidently toward them, smiling, as if they were all good buddies.

Will greeted him.

"I didn't know you were off this period," Ivy said.

"My history class is in the library," he told her. "I'm doing research, can't you tell?"

Ivy laughed lightly, determined to seem as much at ease as he. "What's your topic?"

"Famous murders of the nineteenth century," Gregory replied, pulling out a chair.

"Learning anything?"

He thought for a moment, then smiled and sat down next to her. "Nothing useful. Will, I'm sorry I missed you last night."

Ivy turned to look at Will.

"How about getting together later this afternoon?" Gregory proposed.

Will hesitated, then nodded in agreement. "Celentano's," he said.

"Can I come?" Ivy asked. She caught both of them off guard.

"Oh, I forgot," she said with a casual wave of her hand. "I'm working today."

"Too bad," Gregory said, but his and Will's surprised expressions had told her what she wanted to know. This meeting was business. Gregory was going to pay off Will. At least Will was smart enough to make the exchange in the safety of a public place.

Throughout the conversation, Beth didn't say a word. She watched with wide blue eyes, and Ivy wondered if she could read any of the thoughts behind their faces. She had left her brownie half eaten in its tinfoil.

"If you're not going to finish that, I will," Ivy said, struggling to find normal things to say, working to keep up the pretense that nothing was wrong and she wasn't afraid.

Beth pushed the brownie over to her. While

Gregory and Will set a time to meet, Ivy broke off a piece, then placed what was left of the dessert in front of Gregory.

"What time did you get home last night?" she asked him.

Gregory looked at her silently for a moment and rocked back on his chair. "Let's see . . . nine o'clock, I think."

"Did you hear anything strange outside?"

"Anything like what?" he replied.

"Whining or howling, a cat in pain."

"Did something happen to Ella?" Beth asked.

"Something went after her," Ivy told them.

Will frowned. His old concerned look was getting to Ivy.

"Scraped the fur off in a strip and drew some blood on her right side," Ivy continued. "But there weren't any bite marks. What kind of animal would have done something like that?" she asked, looking directly at Gregory.

"I have no idea," he said coolly.

"Do you know, Will?"

"No . . . no. Is Ella all right?" She heard the slight tremor in his voice, and it almost drew her back to him.

"Oh, sure, she's fine," Ivy said, standing up, tossing her half-finished lunch into a nearby trash barrel. "Ella's a tough little street kitten."

"Just like her mistress," Gregory said, smiling. "Just like her."

15

Ivy couldn't stop thinking about wheels. All day she drew circles with notches in them . . . in her math notebook, on a Spanish quiz, and on a handout in history. They became tractors, snowflakes, strange knobs on a door. Later, at 'Tis the Season, she noticed every item in the store that was round—Christmas wreaths, swimming tubes, and a pincushion made to look like a chocolate-frosted doughnut.

Ivy tried not to think about what was going on at Celentano's and was just as glad when Tristan didn't answer her call. She didn't have to tell him about the blackmail note, she reasoned. It wasn't Tristan who had foolishly trusted Will.

When Ivy got home from work that evening, Maggie and Andrew were out, and Philip was in the family room with Gregory watching a video.

"Did you finish your homework?" Ivy asked her brother.

"Yup. Gregory checked it."

Gregory, playing the role of good and helpful older brother, smiled up at her. Ivy returned the smile, though she tingled with fear at Philip's growing attachment to him. What would Gregory do, she wondered, when he found out that they'd be legally sharing a father? For Gregory, money was status. It was how he controlled the people around him. How would he react if he found out he and Philip might be sharing the Baines fortune?

"Stay awhile," Gregory said to her, gesturing casually to the seat next to him.

"Thanks, but I've got stuff to do upstairs."

She started toward the hall, but Gregory got up quickly and stood in the path Ivy meant to take. "Your mother left a pile of laundry outside your bedroom," he told her. "Maggie said she hoped you had a key. The bathroom door was locked too."

"I have a key."

He leaned close to her and lowered his voice. "She said she hopes you're not doing drugs in there." His mouth twisted up in a grin.

"I'm sure you set her straight," Ivy replied.

He laughed, and she walked past him.

At the top of the steps she pulled the key out of her purse. When she pushed open her bedroom door, she expected the captive Ella to spring out.

"Ella?" She stepped inside the room. "Ella?"

She saw a round lump beneath the quilt on her bed. Ivy dropped her books by the side of the bed, then pulled back the cover. Ella was huddled in a tight ball.

Touching the cat gently, Ivy rubbed her with one finger in her favorite spot around her ears, then stroked her, studying the bare strip on her side. The scratches were beginning to heal.

"You look so frightened, Ella."

The cat slowly got to its feet and limped to the edge of the bed. Ivy quickly reached for her, picking up the paw Ella wouldn't use.

"Oh, my God!" The pink pads on the bottom were pricked and striped with dark blood. When she touched them, they oozed fresh red beneath their drying crust. Ivy scooped the cat up in her shaking arms and huddled over her.

"Oh, Ella, I'm sorry. I'm sorry." She laid her face on Ella's fur, hot tears rolling down. "I locked the door—both doors. I'd never have left you if I thought he could get in."

How did he get in? Ivy wondered. Her bedroom had been his once, so perhaps he had another key. Tonight she'd sleep with furniture against the doors. "Tomorrow when I'm at school, I'll keep you in the car," she promised Ella.

She got up and closed her bedroom door, wondering if Gregory had been lurking outside and enjoying the scene. After cleaning Ella's foot and side, Ivy cuddled her for a long time. The cat purred a little, slowly closing her eyes.

When Ella was sound asleep, Ivy gently laid her in bed. As soon as she put the cat down, her hands began to shake again. She picked up a sturdy chair and positioned it under the knob of the hallway door. After making certain it was secure, she undressed. Maybe a long, hot shower would calm her down.

Ivy locked the door between the bathroom and Philip's room, then switched on the shower radio and turned on the water full blast. For the first ten minutes she was able to push everything out of her mind but the music. But troubled thoughts kept circling at the edge. The wet string with the key hanging on it rubbed against her neck. Ivy squeezed her eyes shut, but she kept seeing images of wheels and hand-printed words, the words of the blackmail note.

At last she shut off the shower and stood still and dripping in the tub. She wondered if Tristan missed the feel of water running over his body. She missed the touch of Tristan. She tried to recall it, but her mind kept jumping back to Will. She focused on Tristan's face, but her mind remembered how it had felt when Will held her hand the day they went back to the train station. She tried to remember how Tristan's hand looked resting on hers, but again she felt Will's touch when he had reached to get the mud out of her hair, when he had laid his hand on hers at lunch to make her look at him.

Ivy thrust aside the shower curtain and stepped out of the tub. Instantly her foot stung as if a hundred small needles had been jabbed in it. She fell back against the

176

tub. Steadying herself, she sat on the edge and gingerly lifted her foot to examine it. Splinters of glass protruded from her foot and sparkled on the bath mat.

Ivy's mind raced, and she rocked back and forth, holding on to her ankle, squeezing it hard. Then she calmed herself and began to pick the glass out of her foot, removing all she could with her hands. After folding over the glass-covered bath mat and setting it aside, she checked the floor, then hopped to the cupboard to get a pair of tweezers.

None of the glass had gone in deeply. It was just enough to make her sore—just enough to rattle her. Ivy made herself work calmly and methodically, then she put on her robe and lifted her foot to look at it again. It was striped and dotted with droplets of blood—just like Ella's.

Suddenly Ivy sank down on the floor. She drew her knees up to her chest. "Tristan!" she cried out. "Tristan, please come! I need you."

She began to sob uncontrollably. "Tristan! Don't leave me alone now. I need you! Where are you? Please, Tristan!"

But he did not come. At last Ivy's sobs softened, her shoulders grew still, and she cried slow, silent tears.

"Aa-hmm."

It was the sound of someone clearing her throat.

"Aa-hmm."

Ivy glanced up and saw a purple mist in front of the vanity mirror.

"I don't know where he is," Lacey said in a brisk, businesslike tone. Then the shimmering purple moved closer to Ivy.

Ivy tried to blink back the tears, but they kept coming. A tissue was plucked from the box and hung in the air in front of her, waiting to be taken.

"Thanks . . . Lacey."

"You look terrible when you cry," Lacey said, and Ivy heard the pleasure she took in that observation.

Ivy nodded, wiped her eyes, then blew her nose hard. "I guess you looked pretty good," she said. "Movie stars always do."

"But I never cried."

"Oh."

"Never sigh, never cry," Lacey boasted. "That was my rule."

"And you kept it?"

"During my life I did," Lacey replied.

Ivy heard the small catch in Lacey's voice. She reached out, accepting another tissue, then asked, "How about now?"

"None of your business," Lacey told her. "Let me see your foot."

Ivy obediently held it up. She felt the tips of fingers gently probing it.

"Does it hurt much?"

"It'll be all right." Ivy lowered her foot and stood up, putting her weight on it slowly. It hurt a lot more than she wanted to admit. "Actually, I'm more worried about Ella. Her paw has been cut up." Ivy told Lacey about the fur that had been shaved from Ella and the lock of her own hair that had been clipped. "By Gregory, I'm sure."

"What a clever guy," Lacey remarked sarcastically. "I guess you got his message: What happens to Ella will happen to you."

Ivy swallowed hard and nodded. "Did you look for Tristan?"

"At Caroline's house. At Will's. At his graveyard condo. He's nowhere—maybe in the darkness again." Lacey sighed, then caught herself doing that and tried to pretend she was clearing her throat again.

"You're worried," Ivy said, opening the door and leading the way into her bedroom.

"About Tristan? Never." The purple mist passed Ivy and stretched out on the pillows across the top of her bed.

"You're worried. I can hear it in your voice," Ivy insisted.

"I'm worried he'll fly off somewhere and I'll get stuck with his job," Lacey retorted.

Ivy sat down on the bed, and Ella raised her head. "It was nice of you to come when you knew I needed help."

"I didn't come for you."

"I know," Ivy said.

"You *know*," Lacey mocked. The purple shimmer sprang from the pillow like the glimmering ghost of a cat. "And just *what* do you think you know?"

"That you care a lot about Tristan," Ivy said aloud. That you're in love with him, she thought.

"That you care so much, you'd help someone you absolutely can't stand and wish would disappear, just to make it better for him."

For once Lacey didn't say anything.

"As soon as I see Tristan again, I'll tell him you came when I called," Ivy added.

"Oh, I don't need anybody scoring points for me," Lacey said quickly.

Ivy shrugged. "Okay, I won't tell him."

Lacey came closer to the bed. Ivy saw Ella's injured paw being lifted up.

"Nasty."

"Lacey"—Ivy's voice shook a little—"can you talk to cats? Can you explain to Ella that I didn't know Gregory had a way of getting in? Could you tell her I would never have left her if I'd known, and that tomorrow I'll—"

"Who do you think I am," Lacey interrupted, "Dr. Doolittle? Snow White? Do you see little *birdies* landing on my hands?"

"I can't even see your hands," Ivy reminded her.

"I'm an angel, and I can no more talk cat than you can."

Ella began to purr.

"But I'll tell you what I can do," Lacey said in a softer voice. "What I'm gonna do. If it works," she added. "It's kind of an experiment."

Ivy waited patiently.

"First, lie down," Lacey commanded. "Relax. Relax! No, wait. Get a candle."

Ivy rose and searched through her desk drawers, at last holding up an old Christmas candle that Philip had given her. "Where do you want it?"

"Somewhere where you can see it," replied Lacey.

Ivy set it on her bedside table and lit it. At the same time she saw Ella get up as if being prodded. The cat limped down to the other end of the bed.

"Now lie down with your feet at this end, next to Ella," Lacey said.

Ivy stretched out on her bed as directed, and the bedroom light clicked off.

"Look at the candle. Relax!" Lacey barked.

Ivy laughed a little. Lacey wasn't exactly a pro at making someone else feel comfortable. But after several minutes of staring at the warm and flickering flame, Ivy did begin to relax.

"Good. Don't fight me now," Lacey said in a quieter voice. "Keep your eyes on that candle. Let your thoughts, your mind, your spirit float toward it, leaving your body behind. Leave it with me so I can do my work."

Ivy watched the flame, watched how it shaped and reshaped itself. She imagined herself like a moth, flying toward the fire, circling it. Then she felt the sole of her foot growing hot. She felt as if a burning hand were wrapped around her foot, and she fought the reflex to pull away. Watch the candle, watch the candle, she told herself as the heat became more and more intense. Just when she thought she couldn't take any more, the burning lessened. There was a cool touch, then a tingling feeling.

"Done."

Lacey's voice was so weak that Ivy had to strain to hear it. Even in the darkness, Ivy could barely see Lacey's shimmer now. She sat up quickly. "Are you all right?"

Lacey didn't answer the question. "Turn on the light," she said, her voice as thin as thread.

Ivy got up to do so and, without thinking, stepped down hard on her injured foot. There was no pain, not even a tingling. She switched on the light, then sat down quickly and lifted up her foot. Her sole was smoother than the palm of her hand, smoother than the sole of her other foot, and without a trace of the cuts. Ella's paw was also healed.

"Yes! Oh, yes!" Lacey congratulated herself. "Lacey, you are good!" she said, but her voice still rasped like an old woman's, and her purple shimmer lay low to the floor.

"Lacey, what's happened to you?" Ivy asked. "Are you okay?"

There was no answer.

"Talk to me," Ivy demanded.

"Tired."

"Tristan," Ivy called softly on the outside, but loudly on the inside. "Please come. Something's happened to Lacey. You have to help her, Tristan. Angels, help Lacey!"

"Just tired," murmured Lacey.

"You shouldn't have tried that. You did too

much," Ivy said, frightened. "I don't know how to help you. Tell me what to do."

"Go. Gregory's in Philip's room now. Go."

Ivy didn't move.

"Take Ella," Lacey said weakly. "Let him see. It'll be fun."

"No. I'm not leaving you like this."

"I said *go!* Make it worth my time."

"Stubborn angel," Ivy muttered. She picked up Ella and reluctantly started toward the door. As she passed through it she heard Lacey say softly, "You're all right, Ivy, you're all right."

"What did you say?" Ivy called back.

But Lacey wouldn't repeat it.

Carrying Ella like a baby over her shoulder, Ivy walked into Philip's room. When Gregory saw her standing in the doorway, his eyes brightened. He's hoping I'll scream like I'm crazy and accuse him, Ivy thought. She smiled at him and saw him glance down. His smile flattened when she padded in comfortably barefoot and without pain.

"Ella wants to say good night," she said. Ella was squirming wildly in her arms, wanting to get as far away as possible from Gregory.

Though Ivy felt bad about restraining Ella, she knew that she could score some points against Gregory, psychological points that might keep her and Ella safe for a while. She purposely kept Ella's shaved flank next to her. The wounds were healed, but the skin was still bare. Sitting on Philip's bed, Ivy drew her feet up next to her so Gregory could see her smooth, bare soles.

She saw the flicker, the momentary puzzlement in his eyes, and then the mask was back in place—the nice-big-brother mask he wore while putting Philip to bed. Of course, he could think of an explanation for her unscarred feet: she had known something was up, she had looked before she stepped out of the shower and avoided the glass.

"I want to give Ella a hug," Philip said.

He reached for her, but Ivy held on tightly to the wriggling cat.

"What's wrong with kitty?" Gregory asked.

"I don't know. I think she wants to play."

Gregory smirked.

"Is that it, Ella?" Ivy asked. "Feeling your oats, girl?" She flipped the cat on her back as if she were going to scratch her tummy.

That's when Gregory saw it, the small foot with its tender pads as pink and smooth as a kitten's. His eyes flicked to Ella's other feet, as if he thought he had forgotten which one he had hurt. Ivy kept the cat on her back, giving Gregory plenty of time to look at her paws. His breathing became shallow. The color drained from his face.

"I want to give her a hug," Philip said again.

"Her, and not me?" Ivy teased, then set Ella in his lap. The cat was off like a shot, running back to Ivy's bedroom, too fast for an animal with an injured paw, too fast for anyone to notice the bare strip of skin on her side.

"Oh, well," Ivy said, leaning over to kiss Philip. "Good night, sleep tight." She brushed past Gregory. "Don't forget to pray to your angels."

The next day Ivy put a box of litter and a pile of blankets in her car and took Ella to school with her. It was clear that whether or not her bedroom doors were locked, Gregory had a way of getting in. Maybe he had a key, or maybe he was good at picking locks. Perhaps there was another way into the attic, she thought, a trapdoor he could climb through that would let him come down again by way of her music room. In any case, she couldn't leave Ella home alone.

Ivy parked at the far end of the school lot, beneath a cluster of weeping willows. The trees would shield the car from both sun and rain, she reasoned, glancing at the clouds rising in the west. She lowered the windows to give Ella some air, but not far enough to allow someone to unlock the car.

"That's the best I can do, cat," she said, and hurried off to homeroom.

Ivy caught up with Beth first period, as they were going into English class. "Any more dreams?" Ivy asked her.

"The same one, over and over. If you don't figure it out soon, I'm going to go crazy."

They both stepped back as people pushed by them to get in the classroom.

"I wish I could talk to Tristan," Ivy said. "I can't reach him."

"Maybe he's working with Will," Beth suggested.

Ivy shook her head, certain that Tristan would not have asked Will for help, but Beth went on. "Will wasn't in homeroom this morning."

"He wasn't?" Ivy tried to stifle a new fear that awakened in her. Why should she worry about Will? He knew what kind of person Gregory was, and he thought he could handle him. He thought he could betray her with no consequences.

"He called me from work late last night," Beth went on. "He was supposed to help me with my computer today, but he said he was caught up in something and couldn't meet me."

Oh, angels, watch over him, Ivy prayed silently. Had Will gotten himself in deeper? Was he working for Gregory now, the way Eric once had? Angels, protect him, she prayed in spite of herself.

"Ladies," Mr. McDivitt called out to them, "the rest of us are doing English. How about you?"

Ivy spent English class, and every class that followed, drawing wheels with notches. And she continually tried to reach Tristan. Each hour of the day seemed to stretch, then collapse like an accordion: minute by minute, the hour dragged itself out, then suddenly was gone, moving them all one hour closer to whatever Gregory was planning next. Ivy longed to climb up on a desk and move the clock's hands ahead, set the wheels in motion.

Wheels . . . clocks, she thought. Clocks had gears—notched wheels—and old clocks, like the one that sat on the dining room mantel at home, had keys to open their casing. Why hadn't she thought of it before? In Beth's dream the wheels were spinning one way, then Ivy reached out and pushed them in the other direction—sending time backward, she thought, sending them into the past. In the past Caroline had lived in the house on the ridge. She could have hidden something in the mantel clock long ago.

Ivy glanced again at the clock on the classroom wall. There were twenty-five minutes left in the last period of the day. She knew her mother would be leaving to pick up Philip from school, and Gregory should still be in class. This was her chance. As soon as written work was assigned, she carried her books to the front of the room. "Mrs. Carson," she said weakly.

Ivy was excused immediately and didn't make the required stop at the nurse's office. Fifty feet from the school door, she made a dash for her car.

A cool autumn rain had moved in and was misting the town. Ivy drove two blocks before thinking to put on her windshield wipers. Her foot was fast and jerky on the clutch, and she started and stopped, impatient with the traffic in the narrow streets. Ella kept trying to climb onto her lap. "Hang on, cat!"

When she finally got to the driveway to the house, she raced to the top, yanked on the parking brake, and got out of the car, leaving the door open. No one was home—at least no one else's car was there. Her hands shook with excitement as she unlocked the house door and turned off the alarm system.

Ivy ran through the kitchen and into the dining room. On the mantel sat the two-foot-high mahogany clock with its beautiful moonlike face and gold pendulum swinging steadily behind painted glass. She had remembered right: there was a keyhole in its casing.

Ivy lifted the string necklace over her head, then reached up with the key and inserted it in the lock. She turned it gently to the left, then the right. The lock clicked, and she opened the clock's door.

She expected to see something immediately. There was nothing, and for a moment she couldn't breathe. Don't be stupid, she told herself. Someone has to wind the clock, someone else has a key—probably Andrew—so nothing's going to be left in plain view. She cautiously reached out and caught the pendulum in midswing, then slipped her other hand in and felt around.

She'd need a stool to reach all the way up into the clock's works. Standing on tiptoe, Ivy moved her fingers slowly up one side of the wood case. She felt an edge, a paper edge. She pulled it gently at first, afraid she'd tear it and leave part of it up in the clock. It was a thick folded edge, like that of an envelope. She tugged on it harder, and it came free.

Ivy stared at the old brown envelope she held in her hands. Then she swiped a dinner knife from the silverware drawer and quickly slit it open.

16

Inside the envelope Ivy found three pages. The first was a handwritten note that was barely decipherable, but Ivy recognized the signature at the end: Caroline's. Beneath it was a letter from the office of Edward Ghent, M.D.—Eric's father, Ivy realized with a sudden jolt. The third page looked like a photocopy of a technical report from a company called MediLabs.

Ivy skipped to the short letter from Eric's father. There were odd spaces between the words and several corrections.

Dear Caroline,

    The enclosed report indicates the situation is as you suspected. As I explained in the office, this type of blood test can prove, in certain instances where there is no match, that a man is not the father. Clearly Andrew is not.

Not Gregory's father? Ivy wondered, then went on.

> The tests cannot prove that Tom S. is the father, only that he is a candidate, but I take it that that was not a question for you.

"Tom S., Tom S.," Ivy murmured. Tom Stetson, she thought, the man at the party, tall and lean and dark-haired like Gregory, the one Tristan said was a teacher at Andrew's college—the man who left roses on Caroline's grave. She finished the letter.

> If I can be of any further assistance, let me know. Of course, this will remain confidential.

Meaning, Ivy thought, that no one else would know who Gregory's father was. No one else, including Andrew? The answer to that question might be buried in the scrawl of Caroline's letter. Ivy read it all the way through.

> Andrew,
> I'm leaving this here for when the right time comes. In the divorce your son sided with you, lied for you, convinced the judge to let him live with you—or was it your money he wanted to live with? And is he really your son?
> Sorry about that.
>
> Caroline

So Andrew didn't know, Ivy thought. And if Gregory knew, he wouldn't want anyone else to. He was counting on the Baines money. Ivy wondered what would happen if Andrew found out that Gregory wasn't really his son. And what would happen now that Andrew had another son, one he was growing very fond of?

Maybe Caroline had guessed what was coming. Maybe she'd realized that this was her chance to get back at both Andrew and Gregory. Ivy could imagine her taunting Gregory. She remembered the day that he'd come from his mother's house extremely upset—Ivy could imagine Caroline threatening to tell all.

Would Gregory have silenced her, killed her for an inheritance?

These letters were enough to take to the police, enough for them to start a serious investigation. Eric had left her what she needed. Angels, she prayed, let Eric rest in peace now.

Then she glanced up at the clock. It showed twenty-seven minutes before three, but she had stopped it with her hand, and at least five minutes had passed. Gregory would be home soon. Ivy moved quickly, starting the swing of the pendulum, closing and locking the clock door. She slipped the key string around her neck and refolded the three sheets of paper, putting them carefully in the envelope. Then she dashed toward the back door.

Outside the mist had become a light drizzle. Ivy

stuck the envelope under her shirt and ran for her car. She drove to the police station, her damp arms covered with goose bumps. At a red light in town, Ivy fumbled through her purse, then dumped everything in her lap, trying to find the card with the name of the detective who had investigated her assault. "Lieutenant Patrick Donnelly," she read from the card, then tossed a lapful of tissues and hair ribbons into the back seat with the cat stuff. That was when Ivy remembered.

"Ella," she called, hoping the cat was under the blankets. "Ella!" At the next light Ivy reached back and felt the old quilt. There was no warm lump. Ivy figured the cat had escaped when she left the car door open. "Stay outdoors, Ella," Ivy whispered. "He can't corner you there."

When she arrived at the station, the desk sergeant took Ivy's name, then informed her that the lieutenant was out. "He'll be back any time now. Anytime now," he repeated, his mild blue eyes watching her as she tore at the edges of the detective's card. "Is there something I can do for you?"

"No." She tore at the card.

"I'll find you someone else to talk to," he offered.

"No, I'll wait," Ivy insisted. The story was too strange and too complicated to tell someone else.

She sat down on a hard bench and stared at the room's olive-colored walls and dreary tile. Directly across from her was a large clock. Ivy watched the minute hand jump from one black dot to the next as she tried to think what she'd say to the detective.

Better leave the angels out, she thought. It would be tough enough to make him take her seriously.

The door of the station swung open, and Ivy looked up hopefully. Two young officers reported to their desk sergeant, turning their backs to her. Ivy got up to ask if someone could telephone Lieutenant Donnelly.

"Expected Pat back by now," the sergeant was saying softly to the other officers as she approached. "He's talking to the O'Leary kid."

The O'Leary kid? Will?

The officers turned around suddenly, and the sergeant's eyes met hers. "Are you sure there's nothing we can help you with in the meantime?"

"You can give this to Lieutenant Donnelly," Ivy said, pulling out Caroline's envelope. She asked for a bigger envelope, then scribbled on it: "I have to talk to you as soon as possible." She wrote down her name, address, and phone number, then sealed Caroline's envelope within. She handed it silently to the desk sergeant and hurried outside. As she sped home Ivy couldn't stop worrying about both Ella and Philip.

When she pulled up in front of the house, she saw only her mother's car in the garage. Good, she thought, Philip was safe, and she'd have a chance to find Ella before Gregory arrived. Ivy took a roundabout route upstairs, passing through the dining room to make sure that she hadn't left behind any signs of her search. The clock was ticking steadily, though it was several minutes slow.

Ivy ran up the center stair two steps at a time. Hearing her mother on her bedroom phone, Ivy stuck her head in the door and gave a half wave, then continued on to her bedroom. The door was wide open, and Ella was not in sight. There were no round lumps in the bed, so Ivy checked underneath, thinking that after all that had happened, Ella might be hiding there. She wasn't, but Ivy noticed that the shoes and boxes under her bed had been pushed to one side, forming a wall.

She studied the wall, then gripped the quilt on her bed. Maybe Gregory had done this to corner Ella the day he cut her paw. Maybe it had helped him trap Ella when he shaved her flank. But there, as part of the wall, were the slippers Ivy had kicked off this morning. She straightened up slowly and saw that the door to her third-floor music room was open. She always kept it closed.

"Ella," she mouthed, the feeling of dread so strong in her she could not speak aloud. She couldn't even walk. She crawled over to the door and saw that the light was on upstairs. Gripping the door frame, Ivy pulled herself up, then slowly climbed the stairs. What had he done to her now? Cut up another foot? Sliced a piece of her ear?

When Ivy got to the top of the stairs, she looked immediately under the piano, then beneath the chairs in the room. Finally her eyes went up to the window, the shadow in it.

"Ella! Oh, no! Ella!"

The cat swung from a rope, dangling from a nail in the low ceiling. Ivy yanked at the rope, then lifted up Ella, but her body was limp. Her head hung down, her small neck broken. Ivy shrieked and shrieked, pressing her face against the dead body of Ella, still soft, still warm. Her fingers moved around Ella's ears, touching her gently as if Ella were just sleeping.

"Ella," she moaned, then started screaming again. "He killed her! He killed her!"

"Ivy! What's wrong?" her mother called.

Ivy struggled to get control of herself. Her whole body was shaking. She clung to Ella, rubbing her face against the cat's soft fur. She couldn't bear to let her go. "He killed her. He killed her!"

Her mother was coming up the steps.

"Gregory killed her, Mom!"

"Ivy, calm down. What did you say?" Maggie asked when she reached the top of the stairway.

"He killed Ella!" Ivy let go of the cat and stood between her and her mother.

"What are you talking about?" her mother asked.

Ivy stepped aside.

"Oh, my—" Her mother's hand went up to her mouth. "Ivy, what have you done?"

"What have *I* done? You're blaming *me?* You still think I'm crazy, Mom? It's Gregory. He's the one behind all this."

Her mother stared at her as if she were speaking another language. "I'll call the counselor."

"Mom, listen to me."

But Ivy could see that her mother was too frightened of what she saw, too afraid of Ivy and what she thought Ivy had done, to listen or understand. Maggie picked up a folded piece of paper that had been left on the piano bench and turned it over and over without looking at it.

Ivy tore it out of her mother's hands, unfolded the note, and read: "I can hurt those you love."

She thrust the paper at her mother. "Look! Don't you understand? Gregory is after me! Gregory killed her just to get to me."

Ivy's mother backed away from her. "But Gregory is out with Philip," she said, "and—"

"With Philip? Where?"

"I'll call Ms. Bryce. She'll know what to do."

"Where?" Ivy demanded, shaking her mother by the shoulders. "Tell me where he took Philip."

Her mother pulled away from her and cowered in the corner. "There's no reason to get so upset, Ivy."

"He'll hurt him!"

"Gregory loves Philip," her mother argued from the corner of the room. She was moving sideways, edging toward the stairs. "You must have noticed how much he's played with him lately."

"I've noticed," Ivy snapped.

"He promised Philip they'd go hunting for old railroad spikes today," her mother went on, "and kept his promise even in this damp weather. Gregory is good to Philip. That's why I told him—though Andrew didn't want me to—I told him yesterday that he and Philip would soon be full brothers."

"Oh, no," Ivy said, sinking back against her stereo.

"I can hurt those you love"—she heard the words as clearly as if Gregory were standing next to her, whispering in her ear. She looked up at her mother and said, "Do you know where they've gone to look for the spikes?"

Her mother was backing slowly down the steps. "By the railroad bridges. Gregory said he could climb up on the old one and get a lot of spikes for Philip." Maggie looked relieved to have reached the bottom of the stair. "You come down now, Ivy. Leave Ella alone. I'll call the counselor. Come down now, Ivy."

Ivy started down the steps, and her mother fled from the bedroom. Ivy waited till Maggie was in her own room calling Ms. Bryce, then she rushed through the bathroom and Philip's bedroom and down the back stairs.

"Tristan, where are you?" she cried, running out to the car. She jammed her key into the ignition.

"Tristan, where are you?"

Ivy took off, her wheels slipping, her door rattling. She opened and slammed it again while she was speeding downhill. As fast as she drove, as dangerously fast as she took the curves on the wet asphalt, she felt as if she would never get there.

"Angels," she prayed, tears running down her face, "don't let him . . . don't let him."

17

As soon as he arrived at the top of the ridge, Tristan knew that Ivy wasn't there. Her car was gone. Maggie was standing at the edge of the driveway, clutching a cordless phone, looking distraught. "I don't care what meeting he's in, I have to speak to him."

What happened? Tristan wondered. Where was Ivy? He was still extremely groggy, like a person who had slept too long and too heavily. When he had fallen into this last darkness, it felt as if a force much greater than he, one more powerful than any he had ever experienced, had forced him over the brink and into the dreamless black.

"It's an emergency!" Maggie was shouting into the phone.

Tell me, Maggie, tell me what happened, Tristan thought.

"Andrew. Oh, Andrew." Maggie closed her eyes

with relief. "It's Ivy—she's gone crazy. She's run off."

Run off where?

"I don't know what started it. She went upstairs and all of a sudden I heard her screaming. I went up after her, up to her music room. She—she killed Ella."

What?

"I said she killed Ella. . . . Yes, I'm sure of it."

Gregory killed Ella, Tristan thought.

"I don't know," Maggie moaned. "I told her Gregory had taken Philip to the bridges to collect railroad spikes."

Now Tristan's mind started clicking. Just before Tristan had fallen into the darkness, Gregory had shaved Ella's flank. Tristan had thought Gregory was just trying to rattle Ivy, but now he recognized it as a warning. Gregory was striking closer and closer.

"I thought I'd calmed her down, Andrew," Maggie said. "I told her how good Gregory was being to Philip. I thought I was handling her right. Then I went to call the counselor, and she ran out. She drove out of here like she was crazy. What should I do?"

Tristan didn't wait to hear anything more. He rushed off toward the bridges, taking the route Ivy would have taken by car. He was fully awake now and felt stronger than he ever had. His mind was moving fast. Did Gregory plan to kill Philip? Was he crazy enough to think he could get away with one murder after another?

Crazy like a fox, Tristan thought. What if this

was a trap? What if it was just a way to con Ivy out to the railroad bridges?

Tristan caught up with her on the winding route that followed the river. He rode beside her in the car, but she was so focused on where she was going that she didn't notice his golden light. A sudden bump from a pothole broke through her concentration.

Pothole! More of them. Watch out. Got to get to the bridges. Find Philip, Tristan thought, until he matched a thought with her and slipped inside. "It's me."

"Tristan! Where have you been?"

"The darkness," he said quickly. "Ivy, slow down. Listen to me. It could be a trap."

"That's what you said about Eric," she reminded him, and drove faster. "Maybe if I had gotten to Eric a little earlier—"

"That's not how it was," he interrupted her, "and you know it. You couldn't have saved Eric."

"I'm going to save Philip," she said. "Gregory's not taking anyone else away from me."

"What are you going to save him with? A gun? A knife? What do you have with you?"

He felt the doubts growing in her mind, fresh fear icing her veins.

"Turn back. Go to the police," he urged.

"I went to the stupid police!"

"Then try Will," Tristan said. "We'll go get Will."

"Will can't be trusted," she replied quickly. "You said so yourself."

"I was jealous, Ivy, and mad about the way he was keeping secrets. But we need him now, and he'd do anything for you," Tristan argued.

He felt Ivy draw back. She was keeping something from him. "What? What is it?"

Ivy shook her head and said nothing.

"He can help us," Tristan persisted.

"I don't need his help. I have you, Tristan—at least I thought I did," she challenged him.

"You know you do, but I can't stop bullets."

"And Gregory can't risk them," Ivy said with confidence. "That's been his problem all along. He's got to do it better than that, sneakier than that. There've been too many deaths now. Too many people close to him have died. He can't get away with a murder that has any evidence attached."

Her certain tone told Tristan that this was a losing battle. She had made up her mind.

"I'll be back for you," he said.

"Tristan?" she called out.

But he raced ahead of her now and came to the bridges almost instantly. The weather had worsened, the light drizzle becoming a cold, slicing rain that swept both sides of the river. A mist rose from the warmer water rushing beneath the bridges. Tristan saw the fog, and yet somehow he could clearly see the parallel bridges it blanketed. Gregory and Philip were not in view. Then Tristan heard voices upriver. They were moving north, in the opposite direction from where Eric had died, where there were no easy paths to walk. He felt like an eagle, targeting the two of them exactly, then dropping down beside them. Something had changed in him since the last deep darkness. His own abilities surprised him.

Gregory was standing with Philip in front of a tiny shack that was well camouflaged by bushes and vines. He pushed open the wooden door, and Philip walked into the ramshackle building without hesitation.

"We'll be like real hunters," Gregory was saying to Philip. "I know where there's a pile of wood. I can pull out some dry pieces and build a fire."

Tristan listened, trying to figure out Gregory's plan. Would he set the building on fire and trap Philip inside? No, Ivy was right: it was too obvious, and Gregory had to be very careful now. Besides, Maggie knew that Philip was out with him.

Philip set down his iron spikes. "I'll help. The spikes will be safe here."

Gregory shook his head. "No, you'd better stay and guard our treasure. I'll go get the wood and be back in a few minutes."

"Wait," Philip said. "I can put a magic spell on our treasure. Then no one will be able to take them and—"

"No," Gregory cut him off.

"But I want to help."

"I'll tell you how you can help me," Gregory said too quickly. "Lend me your jacket."

The little boy frowned.

"Come on, give it to me!" Gregory demanded, unable to hide his impatience.

In response Philip's jaw got that stiff, stubborn look. His eyes narrowed suspiciously.

"I need it to carry the wood in," Gregory explained in a gentler voice. "Then we'll build a good fire and get warm and dry."

Reluctantly Philip took off his red jacket. Then his eyes suddenly widened. Tristan knew that he had been spotted.

"What? What are you looking at?" Gregory asked, whirling around.

Tristan quickly ducked out the door so the boy couldn't see his shimmering light, hoping that Philip understood this silent message.

Philip did. "Nothing," he said.

There was a long silence, then Gregory went to the doorway and glanced outside, but he didn't perceive Tristan.

"I thought I saw a big spider," Tristan heard Philip say.

"A spider won't hurt you," Gregory told him.

"A tarantula would," Philip replied stubbornly.

"Okay, okay," Gregory said, his voice hoarse with irritation. "But there isn't one. Stay and guard our treasure. I'll be back."

As soon as he stepped out of the shack, Gregory closed the door and scanned the surrounding bushes and trees. Satisfied that he was not being observed, he pulled a padlock out of his pocket, slipped it over the rusted latch, and silently locked Philip inside.

"Lacey, Lacey, I need your help. Philip needs your help," Tristan called to her, then passed through the walls of the shack.

Philip greeted him with a bright smile. "How come you're here? How come you were hiding?"

Tristan remained where he was and waited for the little boy to move close to him, then he walked over to the door. Just as he had hoped, Philip followed him. Tristan put his hand on the latch, knowing the boy would see the latch glow. Philip immediately reached out and jiggled the handle.

"I can't open it," Philip said.

Matching that thought, Tristan slipped inside him. "You can't because there's a padlock on the outside of the door. Gregory put it on."

Philip reached for the latch again. As if he couldn't believe it, he kept jiggling and pulling on it.

"Stop. It's locked. Philip, stop and listen to me."

But the little boy started banging on the door with his fists.

"Philip—"

He began to kick the door. Growing desperate, he threw his body against it over and over again.

"Stop! It won't work. And you may need your strength for other things."

"What's going on?" Philip demanded. He was breathing fast, his mouth open, his eyes darting around the room. "Why'd he lock me in?"

"I'm not sure," Tristan said honestly. "But here's

what I want you to do. I'm going to have to leave you, Philip, just for a while. If Gregory comes back before I do and lets you out, run toward the road. Get to the road as fast as you can and try to get the attention of someone driving by. Don't get back in the car with him, okay? Don't go anywhere with him."

"I'm scared, Tristan."

"You'll be all right," Tristan assured him, glad that Philip couldn't probe his mind and know how much he himself feared. "I've called Lacey."

"I've called Lacey," a voice mocked. "And lucky for you she didn't have something better to do."

Philip's face brightened when he saw Lacey's purple mist.

"What kind of mess have you two gotten yourself into?" she asked.

Tristan ignored the question. "I've got to leave. You'll be all right now, Philip," he said, slipping outside of him.

"Not so fast," Lacey spoke silently to Tristan so Philip couldn't hear. "What's going on?"

"I'm not sure. I think it's a trap. I have to find Will," he replied quickly, moving toward the shack walls. "Ivy needs help."

"So when hasn't she?" Lacey called to him, but Tristan was already on his way.

18

Ivy drove toward the double bridges, gripping the steering wheel, leaning forward, straining to see. She flicked on her lights, but the mist absorbed them like pale ghosts. The rain and early fallen leaves made the pavement slick, and at a curve in the road the tires suddenly lost their grip on the road. Skidding sideways, her car slid all the way over to the oncoming lane. Without blinking an eye, she pulled it back in line.

The river, woods, and road went for miles and miles. If Philip and Gregory weren't at the bridges, it would be difficult to search for them alone. Ivy wanted to call Tristan back, but he wouldn't come, he just didn't understand. The weather was getting worse, and there was no time to get the police.

Tristan was right, of course. She didn't have a weapon, unless she could count the rusty nail that rattled around in her cup holder. But she did have a threat: she had left the information with the police. And if Gregory hurt Philip, he'd have a lot more explaining to do.

Ivy suddenly jammed on the brakes and wrenched the steering wheel around, almost missing the turn into the clearing. Her headlights made an arc of light against the trees. Her heart started thumping in her chest. Straight ahead was Gregory's car. They couldn't have gotten far on foot, she told herself.

Ivy parked her car facing the road and left the front door gaping open, but this time for a reason. If she and Philip were chased back, she'd push him in the open door, get in behind him, and lock Gregory out. Now she hurriedly searched the ground for a rock. Finding one, she bent down by the rear tire of Gregory's car and used the rock to drive her rusty nail into the rubber.

Ivy ran through the trees, scrambling up on the railroad track. On either side of her the tunnel of trees closed in, heavy and dripping. She raced along the rails, and suddenly the green tunnel opened out and the parallel bridges hung before her as if suspended in midair.

The fog rising from the river hid their long-legged supports, and only the sound of rushing water proved the river ran fast beneath them. Sections of the bridges continually disappeared and reappeared as wisps of clouds caught on their skeletons like filmy scarves, then floated past. In the rain and mist, it was impossible to see where the old bridge abruptly broke off.

The weather was making it easy for Gregory, Ivy thought. All he'd have to do is lure Philip onto the track with him, then give him an unexpected push. In Gregory's twisted mind, what was one more "accident"?

Ivy focused on the old track, where Gregory was supposed to have collected spikes for Philip. She squinted until her eyes stung, then glanced over at the new bridge. The shifting fog swirled up, and she saw a flash of red. Just as quickly, the clouds covered it again. Then the red waved at her once more from the new bridge—the bright red of Philip's jacket.

"Philip!" she screamed. "Philip!"

She started running down the track of the new bridge. "Stay where you are," she called to him, afraid that if he ran to her he'd trip and fall. But as she got closer she realized it was just his jacket lying on the track. Ivy's heart sank, but she kept going, fearing the worst yet needing to find any clue she could about her brother.

The jacket was soaked by the rain, but there were no rips and only a splatter of mud on the cuffs—no sign of a struggle. For a moment she was hopeful. Of course, there didn't have to be a struggle, Ivy thought. Philip could have been conned into taking off his jacket as part of a game, then quickly pushed. She picked up the jacket and held it in her arms close to her, as she had held Ella.

"Find something?"

She whirled around, nearly losing her balance.

"Hello, Ivy," Gregory said. In the mist he looked like a gray shadow, a dark angel perched on the bridge ten feet away from her. "Hunting for spikes?"

"I'm hunting for my brother."

"Not here," he said.

"What have you done with him?" Ivy demanded.

He grinned and took several steps toward her. Ivy took several steps back, still clutching the jacket.

"Chick, chick, chick," Gregory chanted softly. "Who wants to play chick, chick, chick?"

Ivy glanced toward the far bank, expecting to see a train loom up, as in Philip's nightmare, eager to swallow her.

She turned back to Gregory. "What have you done with him?" she asked again, keeping her voice low, struggling to keep down the hysterical fear that was rising within her.

Gregory laughed softly. "Chick, chick, chick," he said, then took a few steps backward.

Ivy moved with him, her anger overcoming her fear. "You killed Eric, didn't you?" she said. "You were afraid of what he'd tell me. It wasn't an accidental overdose."

Gregory stepped back again. She matched him step for step.

"You killed your best friend," she said. "And the girl in Ridgefield—after you attacked me at home, you killed her as a cover-up. And Caroline. That's how it all started. You murdered your own mother."

Step for step she moved with him, wondering

what kind of game he was playing. Was a train coming? Was that what she heard in the distance?

Gregory suddenly reversed his direction, moving toward her. Ivy backed up. They were two dancers on a tightrope.

"Tristan too," Ivy shouted at him. "You killed Tristan!"

"And all because of you," he said. His voice was as soft and eerie as the twisting shapes of fog. "You were supposed to die, not Tristan. You were supposed to die, not the girl in Ridgefield—"

A train whistle sounded, and Ivy spun around.

Gregory exploded with laughter. "Better say your prayers, Ivy. I've heard tales about Tristan becoming an angel, but no one has seen a shimmering Eric. I hope you've been a good girl."

The train whistle sounded again, higher in pitch, closer. Ivy wondered if she could make it to the other bank in time. She could hear the train itself, rumbling through the trees now, close, already too close to the river.

Gregory was walking steadily backward, and Ivy guessed his plan. He'd keep her on the bridge between him and the train. The girl thought to be crazy enough to throw herself in front of a train once would seem to have tried it again.

As Gregory moved backward Ivy stayed with him. "You've got things wrong," she said. "It was all because of *you,* Gregory. You were terrified of being found out. You were terrified of being left out. Your true father

210

could never give you the kind of money Andrew has."

Gregory's mouth opened a little, and he stared at her. She'd taken him by surprise. They weren't far from the bank now, and he stepped back uncertainly. Ivy inched toward him. If he stumbled, she'd have a chance.

"You didn't think I knew the whole story, did you, Gregory? The funny thing is, the day you killed your mother I never saw you. I never saw past the reflections on the glass. If you'd left me alone, I would never have guessed it was you."

She saw his face darken. He clenched his fists.

"Go ahead," Ivy challenged him. "Come get me. Push me off the tracks, but it's one more murder on your head."

She glanced down. Ten feet more—ten feet more and she'd have a chance, even if she fell.

"Caroline gave Eric a key," Ivy continued, "and Eric left it to me. I found some papers in Andrew's clock."

Nine feet more.

"Some pretty interesting letters from your mother," she told him.

Eight feet.

"And a medical report as well."

Seven.

"I turned them in to the police an hour ago," Ivy said.

Six feet. Gregory stopped. He stood absolutely still. So did Ivy. Then, without warning, he lunged for her.

*   *   *

211

Tristan arrived at Will's just as a dark car pulled away from the house. With his sharpened vision, he saw the man inside: he wondered why the detective who had investigated Ivy's assault was visiting Will.

Will stood alone on his front porch, so deep in thought that Tristan couldn't find an easy way to slip in. He saw a pencil in Will's pocket and pulled it out, but Will didn't notice. Tristan tapped the pencil against a wooden post and wrote his own name with materialized fingertips, underlining it twice, amazing himself with the new strength he felt in his hands.

"Tristan!" Will said, and Tristan slipped inside.

He didn't waste any time. "Ivy needs help. She's gone to the bridges, thinks Gregory took Philip there. It's a trap."

"Have to get my keys," Will replied mentally, and hurried inside.

"No!"

Will stopped and looked around, confused.

"Just run. Run!" Tristan urged.

"All the way to the bridges?" Will argued. "We'll never get there in time."

"I'll get you there," Tristan said. "We can do it faster off the road, out of the traffic." He knew how crazy it sounded, just as he knew somehow it was true. The last darkness had given him more strength than he had ever had, powers that he hadn't yet tested.

"Trust me," Tristan said. "For Ivy's sake, trust me," he pleaded, though he had never completely trusted Will.

Will took off, and they moved together as one. Tristan could feel Will's bewilderment and fear. What was happening to Ivy? What was happening to his own body, taken over by Tristan? What did people see?

"I don't think they see us at all," Tristan said. "But I don't know much more than you."

They were on the winding road now. As they traveled strange voices rose up all around them. Were the voices inside his own head? Tristan wondered. Or was it Will's mind rebelling? Maybe they were human voices pressed together the way space seemed to be compressed as they raced across the landscape.

The voices murmured at first and seemed indistinct, but now they grew louder and clearer—noisy jabbering and clear singing, dark voices threatening and high voices arching over all the others.

"What is it?" Will cried, covering his ears with his hands. "What am I hearing?"

"I don't know."

"What is it? I can't stand it!" Will said, shaking his head as if he could shake the voices out of him.

Tristan was experiencing more than the voices. He was seeing things he had never seen before— scared animals hiding behind trees; jagged rocks, though they were covered completely by leaves; roots buried deep in the ground.

They were at the clearing now, and he saw the tracks behind the wet screen of trees. As they rushed toward the bridges the high voices grew higher and more intense, the low grew deep and furious.

"Demons," Will said, trembling, as they came upon the bridges. "It's demons we hear."

As soon as Gregory lunged for her, Ivy turned and ran. There was no way around him on the narrow bridge. As she started running she saw the headlight of the train, like a small sun brightening the fog, rushing through the trees close to the bridge. She couldn't make it to the other side in time—she couldn't beat out the train. But there was no turning back. She had Philip's bright red jacket. If she waved it, the engineer might see her.

Gregory was gaining on her. The whistle sounded again, and Gregory laughed. He was only a few feet behind her, laughing and laughing, as if they were playing tag in the park. He was insane! He didn't care; he'd die with her as long as he could kill her. With each stride he moved closer—she could see him out of the corner of her eye. In desperation, Ivy threw Philip's jacket on the track behind her. It blew and tangled around Gregory's legs. Gregory stumbled. She glanced back and saw him go down on his knees.

Ivy kept going. She could hear the long rumble of the train and ran as hard as she could toward it. If she put enough distance between herself and Gregory, she could try to find a place to cling to, some fingerhold beneath the track to dangle from.

"Angels, help me!" she prayed. "Oh, angels, are you there for me? Tristan! Where are you?"

"Here, Ivy! Ivy, here!"

There were voices all around her, calling her name. She slowed down. Were they just echoes in her head, the sound of the wind being twisted by her frightened mind? Then she saw that Gregory had stopped, too, listening for a moment, his face shining with sweat, his eyes wide, their gray centers ringed with white.

Then Ivy heard one voice clearly. "Ivy."

She recognized it. "Will!" she exclaimed.

He was running along the opposite track, calling to her. The other voices rose behind it, and a dark fear rushed over her. It's some trick, thought Ivy. It's all part of Gregory's plan.

Gregory started after her again, and Ivy rushed on.

Will was running with incredible speed along the parallel bridge. He had caught up to her and was three steps ahead of her when he reached the end of the old bridge.

"Ivy!" he yelled. "Ivy, over here! Leap!"

She stared at him across the seven-foot gap. All around her voices called and chattered, the high voices ringing in her ears and making her head feel light, the low voices drawing her down in despair.

"Leap!" he shouted, stretching his hands out toward her.

Even if he caught her, there was nothing to keep him from tumbling over the side with her. She'd kill them both.

"Ivy, leap!" It sounded like Tristan's voice.

"Ivy, leap. Ivy, leap," Gregory taunted. He had stopped running. He was walking backward on

215

the track now, watching her, watching the clearing where the train would appear any second, his face flushed and a trickle of blood coming out of his nose. His eyes shone—brilliant, triumphant, insane.

"Tristan!" Ivy called out.

"He's here," Will said. "He'll help us."

But she didn't feel Tristan within her and she didn't see him glowing inside Will.

"Where?" she cried out. "Where?"

"Where, where?" the deep voices mocked. The train thundered onto the bridge.

"Tristan, where are you?" Ivy screamed.

"Reach for her, Will. *Reach for her!*"

Will reached out, and Ivy leaped. For a moment a golden arc shimmered between the two bridges, holding up Ivy and Will. Then they fell onto the old track, clinging desperately to the edge so they wouldn't roll off.

The train rushed along the new bridge, and Gregory started running for the opposite bank. Ivy and Will pulled themselves up and screamed at the train till their throats burned. Their voices were drowned out by a growing wave of dark jabbering, an ominous rumbling of voices so deep they seemed to come from beneath everything that lived.

Ivy and Will watched helplessly as the train bore down on Gregory. He'd never make it. He'd have to try to leap to the old bridge. The voices began to shriek. Ivy held her hands over her ears, and Will gripped her tightly. He tried to turn her head away, but she kept looking.

Gregory leaped, reaching up, his arms flung forward, his fingers reaching out. For a moment he stretched like an angel, then he plunged into the mist below.

The train rushed past him, never slowing. Ivy pressed her face against Will. They held on to each other, barely breathing. The tumult of voices murmured and ceased.

"Chick, chick, chick," one sad voice sang out. "Who's a chick, chick, chick?"

Then all was silent.

19

"One box of tissues," Suzanne said Saturday night. "Help yourself, girls. One large pan of brownies."

"Why are you putting the tissues by us and the brownies by you?" Ivy asked. She, Suzanne, and Beth were sprawled on the floor in the middle of her bedroom.

Beth quickly pulled the brownies closer to her sleeping bag. "Don't worry," she said to Ivy, "I've got the knife."

"Suzanne will use her fingernails," Ivy replied. "Keep the pan between us."

"Now, just a minute," Suzanne said, pursing her lips. They were paler than their usual flame red. "For the last four days I have been thoughtful, caring, polite—"

"And it's really getting to me," Ivy said. "I miss

the old Suzanne. . . . I've missed her for more than the last four days," she added softly.

Suzanne's pouty face changed, and Ivy quickly reached out to touch her friend's hand.

"Uh-oh, tissue time," Beth said.

Each of them reached for one.

"I've cried off more mascara in the last four days," Suzanne complained.

"Let's hit the brownies," Ivy suggested, snatching the knife from Beth and cutting three large ones.

Beth trailed a finger along the inside of the pan, picking up big crumbs as well as her brownie, then grinned at Suzanne. "It's been ages since I've been to a sleepover."

"Me too," Ivy said.

"How long has it been since you've had a good night's sleep?" Suzanne asked Ivy, her eyes still watery.

Ivy moved closer to her friend and put her arm around her. "I told you, I slept all the way through last night."

The other nights had been more difficult for Ivy, but she hadn't had any nightmares. At odd times during the night she would awaken and glance around the room, as if her body, having been on alert for so long, was still conditioned to check that all was well. But the fear she had lived with day and night was gone now, and with it the dreams.

The police had arrived at the bridges almost immediately on Tuesday, Lieutenant Donnelly responding to Ivy's note and to an emergency call for help by

Andrew. They found Gregory on the rocks in the river below and pronounced him dead at the scene. A little while later, Philip was released from the shack.

"How's Philip doing?" Beth asked.

"He looks okay," Suzanne observed.

"Philip sees the world the way a nine-year-old does," Ivy told them. "If he can explain things with a story, he's all right. He's made Gregory into a bad angel, and he believes good angels will always protect him from the bad, so he's okay—for now."

But Ivy knew that sooner or later her brother would be asking a lot of hard questions about how someone could act nice to him and still want to hurt him. He'd ask again for all the details.

By the time Ivy and Andrew left the police station Tuesday night, the facts of the case had been sketched out. The lieutenant said the police would inform the family of the girl in Ridgefield, as well as Eric's and Tristan's parents, regarding the further investigation of the case.

Later that evening the Reverend Mr. Carruthers, Tristan's father, came to the house. He stayed with Ivy and her family for several hours, and remained close by until the memorial service three days later, which he presided over. Now that it was over, both Andrew and Maggie looked fragile and worn, Ivy thought—haunted.

"Of course they do," Beth said, as if she had read Ivy's mind. "They've seen a side of Gregory that they never knew about, and it's horrifying. They're just starting to understand what you've been through. It's going to take them a long time."

"It's going to take us all a long time," Suzanne said, blinking back tears. Then she reached for the kitchen knife. "Do you think there are enough tissues and brownies?"

There's something different about her tonight, Tristan thought as he stared down at Lacey Saturday evening. He found her where he had first met her, lounging on his grave, one knee up, the other leg stretched straight out in front of her. Her spiked purple hair caught the moonlight, and her skin looked as pale as the marble she leaned against. Her long nails gleamed dark purple. But there was something different about her.

In Lacey's face Tristan saw a wistfulness that made him hesitate before speaking to her, some touch of sadness that was new to her or that she usually kept well hidden.

"Lacey."

She looked up at Tristan and blinked twice.

"What's up?" he said, sitting down next to her.

She stared at him and said nothing.

"What were you just thinking about?" he asked gently.

Lacey quickly looked down at her hands, touching fingertip to fingertip, frowning. When she glanced up again, she looked as if she were staring straight through him.

He felt uneasy. "Is something on your mind?"

"Have you been to Gregory's plot?" she asked.

"I just came from—"

"*Puh-lease* don't tell me he's winging around here," she interrupted, waving her hands dramatically. "I mean, I know Number One Director chooses the least likely, but that's pushing it just a *little* too far."

Tristan laughed, glad she was acting like herself again. "I haven't seen a sign of Gregory," he said. "Everything's quiet by his grave and up on the ridge, too."

She dropped her hands. "You've been with Ivy."

"I've been there, but I can't reach her," he said. "Neither she nor Philip sees me, and I can't get inside either of their minds. I need your help, Lacey. I guess you're tired of hearing that, but I need you now more than ever."

She held up her hand, silencing him. "There's something I should tell you, Tristan."

"What?" he asked.

"I can't see you, either."

"What!"

"All I can see is a gold shimmer," Lacey explained, rising to her feet, "the same thing everyone else has been seeing when they look at you." She sighed. "Which means either I'm a living person again . . . *brrrt!*" She made her obnoxious TV game show buzzer sound, only it was a halfhearted effort. "Or you're something angelic far beyond me."

"But I don't want to be!" he protested. "All I want to do is tell Ivy—"

"I love you," Lacey said quickly. "I love you."

Tristan nodded. "Exactly. And that I love her so much I want her to find the love she was meant for."

Lacey turned away from Tristan.

"What can I do?" he asked.

"I dunno," she mumbled.

He reached for her to stop her from pacing, but his hand went right through her arm.

Lacey touched her arm where he had tried to grasp it. "You're way beyond me now," she said. "I can't even guess what's happening to you. Do you have any of your old powers?"

"When I came out of the darkness the last time, I had more powers than ever," Tristan replied. "I could project my voice like you. I could write by myself. I was strong enough to hold up Ivy and Will. Now I don't have the strength to do even simple things. How can I reach her?"

"Pray. Ask for another chance," Lacey said, "though reaching her one last time may take everything you have left."

"Is that how it's supposed to end?" Tristan asked.

"I don't know any more than you do!" Lacey snapped. "And you know how I hate to admit that," she added in a softer voice. "All you can do is pray and try. If—if you don't get through, I'll let her know you wanted to. I'll deliver your message. And I'll check on her now and then—you know, give her some angelic advice."

When Tristan didn't say anything, Lacey said, "All right, so you don't want me giving your chick advice. I won't!"

"Please check on her," he said, "and give her all the advice you want. I trust you."

"You trust me—even if I advise her on love?" Lacey said, testing him.

"Even on love," he said, smiling.

"Not that I know anything about . . . love," she said.

Tristan eyed her curiously. Then he stood up to get a closer look.

"What?" Lacey said. "What?" She backed away from his probing light.

"That's it, isn't it?" he said with quiet wonder. "That's what you were thinking about when I found you. You've fallen in love! Don't deny it. Angels shouldn't lie to each other, and neither should friends. You're in love, Lacey."

"Better dead than never, huh?" she replied. "And now you've got your wish, so you can go on."

"Who is it?" Tristan asked curiously.

She didn't answer him.

"Who is it?" he persisted. "Tell me. Maybe I can help. I know you're hurting, Lacey. I can see it. Let me help."

"Oh, *my!*" Lacey walked a circle around the grave. "Look who's orbiting in the upper realm now."

He ignored the remark. "Who is it? Does he know you're here for him?"

She laughed, then dropped her chin and silently shook her head.

"Look at me," he said gently. "I can't see your face."

"Then we're even," she said quietly.

"I wish I could touch you again," Tristan told her. "I wish I could put my arms around you. I don't want to leave you hurting like this."

Lacey grimaced. "That's about the only way you can leave me," she replied softly, then looked at him with a full and steady gaze, her dark eyes shimmering with his own golden light. "Unless . . . ," she said, "unless *I* leave you first. Good idea, Lacey. No sighing, no crying," she said resolutely.

Then she turned and started walking down the cemetery road.

"Lacey?" Tristan called after her.

She kept on walking.

"Lacey? Where are you going?" Tristan shouted. "Hey, Lacey, aren't you even going to say good-bye?"

Without turning around, she raised her hand and wiggled her fingers in a bright purple wave. Then she disappeared behind the trees.

Like the windows of the sleepy town Tristan had passed through on his way back from the cemetery, like the windows of his parents' house that he had looked through one last time, every window in the big house on top of the ridge was dark. Tristan found the three girls asleep on the floor of Ivy's bedroom: Beth with her round, gentle face bathed in moonlight, Suzanne, her mass of black hair flung like shiny ribbons over her pillow, and Ivy in between her friends, safe at last.

What the girls didn't know—or at least had pretended not to notice—was that Philip had crept into Ivy's bedroom and was asleep now in her bed, his head at the lower end where he could listen to their secrets. Tristan touched him with his golden light. Only Ella was missing from the quiet scene, he thought.

He sat for a long time, letting the peace of the room seep into him, reluctant to disturb Ivy's sleep, reluctant to bring the time left between them to an end. But it would end, he knew that, and when the sky began to lighten, he prayed.

"Give me one last time with her," he begged, then he knelt beside Ivy. Focusing on the tip of his finger, he ran it along her cheek.

He felt her soft skin. He could touch her again! He could sense her warmth! Ivy's eyes fluttered open. She looked around the room, wondering. He brushed her hand.

"Tristan?"

She sat up, and he pushed back a tumble of golden hair.

Her lips parted in a smile, and she reached to touch her hair where he had touched it. "Tristan, is it you?"

He matched that thought and slipped inside.

"Ivy."

She rose quickly and walked to the window, wrapping her arms around herself. "I thought I'd never hear your voice again," she said silently. "I thought you were gone forever. After that moment on the bridge, I didn't see your light anymore. I can't see it now," she told him, frowning and gazing down at her hand.

"I know. I don't understand what's happening, Ivy. I just know that I'm changing. And that I won't be back."

She nodded, accepting what he said with a calm that surprised him. Then he saw her mouth quiver. She trembled and looked as if she would cry out loud, but she said nothing.

"I love you, Ivy. I'll never stop loving you."

She leaned against the window, looking out on a pale and glittering night. She looked through tears.

"I prayed for one more chance to reach you," he said, "to tell you how much I love you and to tell you to keep on loving. Someone else was meant for you, Ivy, and you were meant for someone else."

She stood up straight. "No."

"Yes, love," he said, softly but firmly.

"No!"

"Promise me, Ivy—"

"I'll promise you nothing but that I love you," she cried.

"Listen to me," Tristan pleaded. "You know I can't stay any longer."

The pale, glittering night was raining now, and fresh tears gleamed on her cheeks, but he had to leave.

"I love you," he said. "I love you. Love him."

Then Tristan slipped out and saw her standing at the window in the early-morning light. He stepped back and watched her as she knelt down and rested

227

her arms and face on the sill. He stepped back again and saw her tears dry and her eyes close. When he stepped back a third time, Tristan thought the sun had risen behind him, shattering the pale night into a thousand silver fragments.

He turned suddenly to the east, but the brilliant circle of light was not the sun. There was no knowing what it was, except that it was a light meant for him, and Tristan walked swiftly toward it.

20

Ivy awoke with the sun in her eyes. Before she remembered Tristan's visit, and before Beth said drowsily, "I had a dream last night that Tristan came," Ivy knew that he was gone. It wasn't a feeling she could explain, just a clear sense that he was no longer with her and wouldn't be back. The struggle to hold on to what they had, the longing to reach back in time for Tristan, and the dream of living in another world with him had ceased within her. She felt a new kind of peace.

Maggie, Andrew, and Philip were up and out of the house early that Sunday. The girls had a leisurely brunch, then Suzanne and Beth gathered their belongings and carried them out to Beth's car. Suzanne waited till then to ask the question Ivy had expected several times the previous night.

"I've been good," Suzanne began. "All last night and

this morning I haven't said one thing I shouldn't have."

"You ate two brownies you shouldn't have," Ivy reminded her. She watched with amusement as Beth caught Suzanne's eye and made quick cutting signs across her throat. But Suzanne would not be silenced.

"Beth told me that if I brought this up, she'd stuff a purseful of paper in my mouth."

Beth threw her hands up in the air.

"But I've got to ask. What's going on with you and Will? I mean, he saved your life. Am I right?"

"Will saved my life," Ivy agreed.

"Then what—"

"I told Suzanne that you just needed some time to sort things out," Beth intervened.

Ivy nodded.

"But he's totally hooked on you!" Suzanne said, exasperated. "He's head over heels in love—he has been for months."

Ivy didn't say anything.

"I hate it when she gets that stubborn look on her face," Suzanne complained to Beth. "She looks just like her brother."

Ivy laughed then—she guessed she and Philip did share a mulish streak—but she refused to say anything more about Will.

After her friends left, Ivy walked toward Philip's tree house, pausing on the way at the patch of golden chrysanthemums where Ella was buried. She brushed the flowers with her fingers, then moved on. Beth was right, there was a lot to sort out.

Tuesday night she had told the police everything she knew about the case against Gregory—everything but Will's attempt at blackmail. Against her better judgment, Ivy had kept quiet about the note she had found in Gregory's room.

Tuesday night she had succeeded in convincing herself that the police already knew about Will. She had reasoned that they traced the blackmail money when Will deposited it. That's why Donnelly went to Will's house, she told herself now as she climbed the rope ladder of the tree house. But Ivy knew that in the end she had to tell the police about the note. The danger of keeping big secrets had been made all too clear by Caroline's life and death.

She reached the top of the ladder and walked the narrow bridge to the other tree. Brushing aside some leaves, she sat down on the wooden floor. Far to the north, she could see a small strip of the river, a peaceful snippet of blue ribbon. Lying back, she stared up at the tiny patches of sky—not much more than blue stars now—but soon, with the falling leaves, it would be the only roof the tree house would have. That's all right, she thought. The sky was the angels' roof, too.

Angels, take care of Will, she prayed. It was the best she could do for him now. She couldn't trust him. And she could never love someone who had betrayed her as he had. Still, her heart went out to him. Angels, help him, please.

"Hey, is there a doorbell to this house?"

Ivy jumped at the sound of Will's voice, then

quickly rolled over on her stomach to look down at him through the slits between the boards. "No."

He was silent for a moment. "Is there a knocker?"

"No." Her mind raced—or was it her heart? She wished she could think of a clever line to turn him away. She wished he didn't make her ache inside.

"Maybe there are some magic words?" he said.

Ivy didn't reply. Will backed up in the grass, trying to see into the tree house. She lifted her head and looked down over the edge at him.

"If there are magic words, Ivy, I sure wish you'd tell me what they are, because I've been wondering for a long time, and I'm just about ready to give up."

Ivy bit her lip.

"You know," Will continued, "when two people narrowly escape falling to their deaths, they usually have something to talk about. Even if they hadn't met before that moment, they usually have something to say to each other afterward. But you haven't said anything to me. I've been trying to give you some time. I've been trying to give you some space. All I want is—"

"Thank you," Ivy said. "Thank you for risking your life. Thank you for saving me."

"That's not what I wanted!" Will replied angrily. "Gratitude is the last thing I—"

"Well, let me tell you what *I* want," Ivy shouted down at him. "Honesty."

Will looked up with a bewildered expression. "When haven't I been honest?" he asked. It was as if he had totally forgotten about the blackmail. "When?"

"I found your note, Will. I know you blackmailed Gregory. I didn't tell the police yet, but I will."

He frowned. "So tell them," he said, his voice rising with frustration. "Go ahead! It's old news to them, but if you've got the note, it's one more piece for the police files. I just don't get—" He started walking away from the tree house, then stopped. "Wait a minute. Do you think— You couldn't really think I did that to make money, could you?"

"That's usually why people blackmail."

"You think I'd betray you like that?" he asked incredulously. "Ivy, I set up that blackmail—I got the Celentanos to help me out, and I videotaped it—so that I had something to take to the police."

Ivy sat up and moved closer to the edge of the platform.

"Back in August," Will said, "when you were in the hospital, Gregory called and told me you had tried to commit suicide. I couldn't believe it. I knew how much you missed Tristan, but I knew you were a fighter, too. I went to the train station that morning to look around and try to figure out what had gone through your head. As I was leaving I found the jacket and hat. I picked them up, but for weeks I didn't know how or even if they were connected to what had happened."

Will paced around, bending over and picking up small sticks, breaking them in his hands.

"When school started," he said, "I ran across some file photos of Tristan in the newspaper office. Suddenly I figured it out. I knew it wasn't like you

233

to jump in front of a train, but it was just like Eric and Gregory to con you across the track. I remembered how Eric had played chicken with us, and I blamed him at first. Later I realized that there was a lot more than a game going on."

"Why didn't you tell me this before?" Ivy asked. "You should have told me this before."

"You weren't telling me things, either," he reminded her.

"I was trying to protect you," she explained.

"What the heck do you think I was doing?" He threw down the sticks. "I figured that Eric died because he was going to spill the beans. I didn't know why Gregory wanted to kill you, but I figured if he'd murder his best friend, he'd go after you no matter what the risk. I had to distract him, give him another target, and try to get something on him at the same time. It almost worked. I gave the tape to Lieutenant Donnelly Tuesday afternoon, but Gregory had already laid his trap."

He paused, and Ivy moved to the very edge of the platform, dropping her legs over the side, hanging on tightly to the rope that dangled next to her.

"You thought I'd betray you," Will said, his voice sounding hollow and incredulous.

"Will, I'm sorry." She knew from his tone that she had hurt him deeply. "I was wrong. I really am sorry," she said, but he was walking away from her.

"I made a mistake. A big one," she called after him. "Try to understand. I was so mixed up and afraid. I thought I had betrayed myself when I trusted you—and betrayed Tristan when I fell in love with you. Will!"

Grasping the rope, she dropped over the side, then swung free of the tree house. But Will had turned back a moment before. She landed on top of him, and they rolled together to the ground.

They lay there for a moment in a heap, Ivy on top of Will, neither of them moving.

"Nice catch," Ivy said. She was trying to laugh, but all she could do was tremble. She was so afraid he'd get up, dust himself off, and walk away. Why shouldn't he?

"You fell in love with me?" Will asked.

She looked into his deep brown eyes, eyes that shimmered with hidden light, then she saw a smile spreading across his face. His arms encircled her, and she relaxed against him, her face close to his. "Love you, Will," she said softly.

"Love you, Ivy." He held her close and rocked her a little. "You know," he said, "it's a good thing this didn't happen before. If I had known how heavy you were, I would never have reached for you."

"What?"

"Without an angel around, I'd have been a goner," he said.

Ivy pulled herself up abruptly.

Will laughed. "Okay, okay, that was a lie. But this is the truth. The angels will swear to it," he said, then pulled her down for a kiss.

About the Author

Elizabeth Chandler has written picture books, chapter books, middle grade novels, and young adult romances under a variety of names. She lives in Baltimore, and loves stories, cats, baseball, and Bob—not necessarily in that order.